'Hal, what's the point of this?' Nina asked edgily. 'We've been out of each other's lives for a long time now. We won't meet again. Don't you think it would be better just to forget about the past and leave the present alone? We don't know each other any longer.'

Hal stood lounging with a casual animal grace. He looked completely relaxed, while there was an underlying tension in her that felt as though it might twist her shoulders, her neck, and the whole of her spine into knots. She felt threatened by him, dominated by his height, his attitude, his sheer male presence.

'That's not true. There is a point to all this, even if you don't see it. I don't like untidy endings, but you left everything hanging in the air—no explanations, nothing—and I'd like to know why?'

'You never bothered to find out before, when it mattered!' she flashed at him. 'We're not in one of your damn plays, Hal! There's no neat knitting up of the plot at the end—happy-ever-after marriages, and people reunited with long-lost children. . .' Her voice broke on something like a sob.

Another book you will enjoy
by LUCY KEANE

FALSE IMPRESSIONS

Mad, bad and dangerous to know—that was how Bianca saw the artist who accused her of criminal forgery and imprisoned her in his Florence apartment. But then she found this man had the power to turn her world upside-down—and that love need not be a fake. . .

MASK OF PASSION

BY

LUCY KEANE

MILLS & BOON LIMITED
ETON HOUSE 18–24 PARADISE ROAD
RICHMOND SURREY TW9 1SR

First published in Great Britain 1990
by Mills & Boon Limited

This edition 1990

ISBN 0 263 76740 X

Set in 10 on 11½ pt Linotron Times
01-9007-52167
Typeset in Great Britain by Centracet, Cambridge
Made and printed in Great Britain

CHAPTER ONE

NINA let the movement of the sea gently drift her face down over the pebbles while she held her breath to watch the tiny shoals of silver and black fish that infested the shallows. She thought she could be happy floating like that forever in the clear, sunwarmed waters of the Aegean, but soon she would have to head back across the cliffs towards the little harbour where she was staying.

Then, feeling the smooth stones against her naked body, she sat upright, streaming water. The beach was usually deserted, and there hadn't been anyone around when she had tossed her bright pink one-piece aside and gone in to swim. Nude bathing was frowned upon by the local Greeks, and she was careful not to offend them.

The first thing she became aware of, through the blur of sea-water, was that her swimsuit wasn't where she had left it. She smiled to herself—it was just as well there was no one about. She felt fully relaxed—almost contented. It had taken a little longer than usual this time for the island to work its old magic on her, and it was a pity there was only one afternoon left, but in three weeks she had felt the tensions created by a pressured, work-filled existence gradually ease away.

She stood up, water dripping from the long, straight, lint-white strands of her hair, down her tanned back and firm breasts, and streaking her slender brown thighs. She blinked quickly to clear the water from her eyes. There was a pine-scented breeze, as always, blowing from the land. Although there was no tide, the suit might have been blown along the shore, or into the sea where it would have drifted slowly with the wind.

Gathering back wet hair from her face, she turned to discover with a sense of shock that there was someone beside her. A tall, dark man with a piratical beard and one glittering gold and turquoise earring, holding out something fuchsia-pink in his hand. His own minimal clothing—jeans and espadrilles—seemed to emphasise her nakedness, and his eyes assessed her body.

It wasn't easy to make her blush these days. At twenty-six she had learned to assume an outward coolness, at least, that was seldom disturbed, and this man didn't strike her as a local Greek despite his dark colouring. He was too lightly tanned, and too tall and well-built for the smaller, stocky islanders. She scarcely gave him a second glance. She wasn't going to let some stranger spoil that wonderful feeling of inner contentment.

'This is yours, I think?' His voice was deep and somehow disturbing, awakening something in her that she didn't have time to identify before she held out her hand for the suit. It was dripping with sea-water. Her eyes coolly acknowledged his only when she couldn't avoid them any longer—and that instant the impersonal, dismissive words of thanks she was about to offer flew right out of her head.

This tall, dark man with his piratical earring and closely trimmed beard was no stranger. She caught her breath at the heart-stopping sense of shock that was a physical blow, and stared up into the handsome face, those dark eyes, as though time had played some impossible trick on her. For an endless intense moment, it was as though the last five years of her life had never been—five long years in which she had tried to destroy all the deepest feelings she had ever had. And then, despite those years and everything that had led up to them, she was conscious of a sudden release of joy that flooded through every vein in her body.

'Hal!' she said, scarcely above a whisper.

Something that flickered in his eyes told her he had read that unexpected reaction in her. The finely shaped mouth curved into a practised smile that instantly woke far too many memories best forgotten.

'Nina.' His deep voice an assault on the senses in itself. 'I'd remember those eyes anywhere!'

Then, before she could guess his intention or voice a protest, he had stepped so close to her that he had only to draw her fractionally towards him by her naked shoulders to kiss her on the lips.

Momentarily everything blurred round her, and she jerked back from the unexpected contact, her heart almost turning somersaults. She had thought she had managed to persuade herself she had forgotten Hal Crayle. . .or everything that had mattered about him. It hadn't seemed so difficult after a while, with enough determination, but the brief touch of his lips—although no lover's kiss—told her that the past was not so easily buried. A confusion of emotions overwhelmed her. She didn't know what to say.

Almost immediately he released her. She stepped back unsteadily on the pebbles and tried to gather her wits. It struck her belatedly that there had been no surprise in his eyes when he'd greeted her—he had known already who she was. And that kiss was an actor's greeting—after so long it must surely have been calculated; you didn't greet *anyone* you hadn't seen for five years like that! Let alone. . . All the old unhappiness, the old resentments she thought she had successfully buried, came flooding back. The kiss must have had its own hidden malice. Their parting had been too abrupt, too final, for this greeting to have been casual friendship. He had hoped to provoke some further reaction. That fleeting sense of joy had caught her unawares, and he had seen it.

But she was no longer the vulnerable and immature girl she had been when they had known each other all those years ago. The unexpected meeting—Hal, after all this time!—had thrown her off balance, and that the greeting was somehow staged caused her a brief pang of unaccountable disappointment. But she wasn't going to let him see it all. Now she was well able to give as good as she got.

'Hal. What brings you to this obscure island—*resting*?' She managed to surprise even herself with the cool bite she put into the words. In acting circles the word was a polite term for 'out of work'.

He was visibly startled, and stepped back, to her relief increasing the distance between them, holding one hand up in a mock gesture that asked for a truce—a beautifully fluid actor's gesture, as ever.

'Hey, cool it, will you? Couldn't we observe a few of the social niceties before we pick up where we left off?' He still had that lovely, effortless, well-modulated voice that had used to send shivers down her spine as a romantic teenager. But now she was old enough to remind herself of the training and calculation behind its use.

Ignoring the implications of his remark, she glanced round the little cove, deliberately choosing to break the tension that was building between them despite her.

Why him? she was thinking. Why here of all places? She was acutely aware of his eyes on her and of the fact that she was still naked.

The high, rocky slopes of the hills were slanting with afternoon light, and the tamarisk trees, a dusky green, feathered in the wind. It was still the same beautiful island she had visited for the last three years, but, ominously, it was as though he had suddenly changed its perspective for her. She repressed a little shiver.

'I'd better find my clothes,' she said, as casually as she could. The only way to handle the situation was to treat him as some chance-met stranger, although her heart was still beating so erratically that she felt as though it would jump out of her chest.

What on earth could they have to talk about after five years? If only he would go! He had always had a good stock of exit lines. Surely there could be no interest on either side in the conventional 'How are you? What are you doing now?' routine. He could have no real interest in what she had done with her life since they had split up; he had had little enough when they had been together, she reflected with a sudden bitterness, obsessed as he had been by his own career. Since then it was only by chance that she had seen his name on theatre reviews or TV programmes; she had deliberately avoided looking for it. Her interest in Hal, and in the theatre, was a firmly closed chapter in her life.

'If your clothes are a pair of shorts and a T-shirt, they're under a pile of stones.'

'You have been busy.' She sounded as offhand as she could. Think of him as just another tourist, she told herself a little desperately. He won't want to prolong this, anyway. 'Thank you.' Their eyes met briefly—her own a brilliant aquamarine with darker flecks—eyes he said he had remembered.

He sat down beside the heaped clothing, and watched her while she slipped on the loose shorts. 'Your figure has improved since we last met,' he said approvingly. The personal remark disconcerted her, as did the fact that he felt free to watch her—that was a lover's right he had lost long ago, not just the casual appraisal of a stranger—but she hid it behind the light sarcasm.

'You're too kind. So has yours.'

She glanced down at him, her hands lifted to her hair. Even sprawled on the stones, he had a lithe actor's grace. She couldn't help thinking that five years had been kind to him—in the past he had always been a little too thin and too angular for real handsomeness, despite the makings of remarkable good looks. Now the lightly tanned shoulders were clothed with muscle, and the moulding of his ribs, and thighs under the jeans, suggested strength and agility. He was, if anything, far more dangerously attractive on a purely physical level than he had been then. The classically regular features—straight nose and firm jawline—were familiar, but the closely clipped Elizabethan pirate's beard accentuated a powerful masculinity that hadn't been so evident before.

He laughed, easing by just a fraction the latent hostility she could sense between them. He leaned back on his elbows, first scooping two little indentations into the heaped pebbles for comfort. He had a deep, warm laugh. She remembered that too, too well.

She put on the T-shirt, which hung about her like an old man's vest, emphasising the slender lines of her body, and picked up the butterfly clip from the beach where she had tossed it, to pin up the long, wet, flaxen strands of her hair. She was determined to make no effort to encourage the interview—with so much that would have to be left unsaid, there was no point merely making conversation. But, before she could find any suitably dismissive comment, he asked, 'So, what are you doing here of all obscure places? I thought it must be about the smallest, least tourist-haunted island in the Aegean—I was even hoping for just me and a few goats. I certainly didn't expect to be bumping into a beautiful and mysterious woman from my past.'

It was a compliment—but there was a sting in the tail. Yes, she had been mysterious all right: she had never had a chance to explain why she had left him. But never once, through all those first long and agonising months, had he given her one.

I'm on holiday,' she replied shortly. 'I was here last year, and for the two summers before that.'

'Then you'd recommend it as a haven for worn-out actors?'

'It's peaceful.'

He gave her a quick, thoughtful look, but she wasn't prepared to add anything. What was the point? This meeting should never have happened. It was a sort of time-slip—only to call it that would amount to admitting she could still feel the same about him, and that wasn't true, even though that first moment of greeting had taken her breath away.

She had never thought she would see him again, and for too long in those early days she had wasted futile energy in telling herself she never wanted to. It had been a lie then, of course. She knew she had been deliberately building up a distorted image of him that would make separation from him easier to bear. She had built it on the doubts that had crept in during those last, testing weeks they had been together—it was a time when she had begun to question everything about him, even the love he had so often professed.

And time had proved her right to question that: what was love worth from someone who had put his own ambitions before everything, and who when she left him hadn't even made an effort to find out where she had gone?

Gradually the pain had lessened, and her passionate rejection of Hal Crayle and everything he stood for had seemed to dwindle into genuine indifference. Their paths would never cross in future, she had told herself. Why continue to agonise in case they did? It was pointless.

Now she wondered what had brought him to speak to her. If he had recognised her before he approached her, he could easily have avoided her. Had he been watching her long? Had he perhaps recognised her from the moment he first stepped on to the beach? If his calculated actor's greeting had been intended to take the ground from under her feet, he had certainly succeeded. And now she wasn't quite sure how to continue the scene. With Hal somehow it had always been a question of playing scenes.

'I'm on holiday too, though you haven't asked. And thank you, yes, I am having a nice time.' His words had an undercurrent of sarcasm, but she didn't want to be rude to him—she couldn't risk opening up old wounds. If only he had never seen her! She would have gone out of her way to avoid him had she recognised him first.

'I'm not "resting", as you so succinctly put it,' he went on, ignoring her silence. 'I've got too many lines to learn. Would these be your flip-flops, by the way? They don't look as though they're going to last much longer. It's quite a distance between the harbour and here. Have you been across to the other side of the island? It's not far as the crow flies, and there's a beautiful little mountain village over there, above the sea. Only one taverna with about three guest rooms and a splendid view. Makes up for the hardness of the beds—but, as you say, very peaceful.'

She was slipping her feet into the flip-flops as he spoke, noting the frill of rubbery substance round the edge, and the fact that the thong was wearing away from the sole. She supposed he must have come across from the village he spoke of, though she wasn't going to show any interest. All the time she was wondering, What's he trying to get out of this?

'I know it.' Then she added, 'It might be you and the goats after all—even one tourist leaving this island makes a difference. I'm catching the ferry for Piraeus tomorrow, and then flying home from Athens.'

She hoped that would tell him effectively that there wasn't much point in pursuing any sort of relationship with her, and he might as well give up now. But it didn't have any immediate effect—he was obviously waiting for her.

'Shall we walk back?' Again the actor's gesture, this time the one that said 'This way, my lord' or 'After you, my lady'. 'I'd like to find out what you've been up to for the last five—or is it six?—years.'

She rolled the swimsuit into a ball and then squeezed it, outwardly intent on what she was doing. Inwardly, she was struggling not to feel hurt by the casual inaccuracy. Could he really not remember?

'It seems longer,' she replied offhandedly, determined to give nothing away to him.

She folded up the beachmat and secured the tapes, taking her time.

He held out a hand. 'Shall I carry that?'

It was no more than politeness—another thing she remembered about him—an ingredient of that fatal charm that seemed to be able to win over even the most difficult of old ladies, or crustiest of elderly colonels. Virtually everybody, in fact—except her mother.

She shook her head. 'I can manage.'

He waited for her to start walking, standing as he had been trained to do in that relaxed attitude of a man at ease with his body. The turquoise gleamed against the blue-blackness of the slightly overlong hair, and beard. Nina was finding it hard to keep up a defensive pose that required such pointedly casuual replies. It went against her friendly nature to be so rude to him, and she would never have been so offhand with a stranger. But she was still reeling from the shock of the encounter, and, although five years had taught her to develop an outer shell and to act what she couldn't genuinely feel, she was finding it hard to keep up.

Perhaps, when neither of them could utter a sentence that wasn't loaded with some hidden meaning, her only real defence lay in attack.

'You're still in the theatre?' she asked, as they started up the track that led away from the beach. She knew very well that he was, but, if he could so easily dismiss every long year that had passed since their relationship had come to its abrupt end, then she could surely 'forget' how much his passionate involvement with the stage had meant to him. They had always known how to hurt each other.

He shot her a quick, assessing look. It wasn't lost on him, then.

'I do turn my hand to scene painting and sewing on

the general's braid from time to time, but I think it wouldn't be overstating to say yes.'

His sarcasm told her she had scored a point. No actor in professional theatre would ever be concerned with such menial jobs.

'I hadn't seen your name anywhere lately, that's all,' she said dismissively. Would he suspect from that reply that she had sometimes looked for it?

The path was treacherously uneven. Spiky low branches of aromatic sage sprouted between the rocks, and there were scratchy dried thistles to be avoided. Underfoot, the rocks had split like slate, their surfaces covered with loose shale.

Nina had always loved the heavy scent of the pines that grew along the cliff-top, all leaning one way from the constant wind. Now she climbed slowly, regretting one of the last walks of her holiday. By opening a door into her past, Hal's unexpected appearance had suddenly destroyed the peace of the island for her. She concentrated on the fragile flip-flops, hoping that he would grow impatient, and bring this ill-judged encounter to an end.

He was climbing just ahead of her, and, when once or twice the soles of her shoes slipped on the shale, he turned quickly. She didn't look up, though aware of his scrutiny. She was used to compensating for the oddities of her flimsy footwear, and the path would even out soon into a smooth cliff-top walk before the tricky descent into the harbour. If she walked slowly enough he would abandon her long before they got to that last goat track. He had never been patient.

He waited for her to reach the top of thc ascent to stand beside him. She hoped he would decide to go ahead at his own pace, but he walked on at her side.

'So what have you been doing all this time?' he

asked. He wouldn't be able to deduce much from looking at her, she reflected. Just another tourist in T-shirt and shorts.

'I run a tutorial college in Cambridge.'

'Clever old you!' There was surprise in his voice, but no very obvious irony.

OK, she thought defensively, you were the one at university while I didn't even finish my business course, but whose fault was that? Hal of all people, had no right to criticise. He had taken up almost every waking minute of her life. Her parents' disapproval and anger with her had been a different matter—she had long ago admitted to herself that they might have had some justification for their attitude towards him.

She wasn't going to let him get away with a remark like that, though. Underneath, it still hurt.

'Why do you sound surprised?' she asked coldly.

His reply was vague. 'Oh, I suppose I never imagined you doing anything so scholarly. What happened to all that fire? Once you'd given up that course, I thought you'd do something artisitic in the end—perhaps still connected with the theatre.'

She shrugged, determined to dismiss the topic. 'No. I was never as keen on it as you were.'

'Hm. I remember a time when you were every bit as keen—what about when we first met? I also remember a critic who thought you were the best Juliet he'd seen for years. "Ethereally fair. . .like an angel",' he quoted, half mockingly.

'That just meant he liked the colour of my hair,' she said quickly, not wanting to be reminded of the dreams that the newspaper review had encouraged.

'But what about your "depths of feeling" and "intensity of controlled passion surprising in such a young actress"?'

She was astonished that he remembered the wording of the review she had been so proud of—could it mean that his memory of their shared past was more acute than some of his casual remarks had implied? She of course had known it by heart, having cut it out of one of the national dailies that had written up their student performances in *Romeo and Juliet*—the play they had taken on an unexpectedly successful student tour. She must still have the cutting stored away somewhere.

It had been that play that had brought them together. Hal, a 'mature student' at twenty-four, had been studying at Oxford University. Nina, only eighteen, had been taking a business course at a local polytechnic, and her interest in acting had led her to join in some of the student drama activities that year. Hal had been the star of the university dramatic society, and the star of that production of *Romeo and Juliet*, although he hadn't played the leading role.

'I thought you were the one who had got all the good newspaper reviews,' she said coolly. 'It was just as well Shakespeare killed off your character in the third act, or Romeo wouldn't have had a chance.'

She could remember the young man, David, who had played Romeo. He had been good-looking and a reasonably competent actor—but completely outshone for the entire first half of the play by his quixotic and quarrelsome companion Mercutio, played by Hal.

That hadn't been the only area in which Hal had carried off the prizes, she remembered painfully. Tall, handsome, angular and surpisingly agile, he was spellbinding on stage, and could hold an audience even then by the sheer beauty of his voice. But off-stage too his intelligence and magnetic personality could still weave its spells—no wonder every girl involved in the play had been in love with him.

She had found out afterwards that most of the cast had been laying bets on the chances of various actresses ending up in his bed, and that she herself had quickly become a favourite, despite her wary attempts to keep him at arm's length. She had been just as dazzled by him as all the others, of course, but frightened of her own inexperience with a man who seemed older than all her friends. She had known her unusual looks attracted a lot of attention, but looks alone wouldn't be enough to draw someone like Hal. Surely he couldn't be serious about someone as young and unsophisticated as she was, she had told herself. Not when he could have had any girl he wanted.

There had been a good deal of feeble wit among the cast at the expense of poor Romeo—David, at nineteen so very much younger than the confident and glamorous Hal, had definitely had a weakness for her, and his kisses for Juliet had become more enthusiastic with each performance. But it had taken Mercutio, waiting one night off-stage in the wings for their final bow, to show her what kisses really meant.

She still remembered vividly how, as she had acknowledged the storm of applause, she had been conscious of nothing and no one but Hal, smiling and bowing with practised ease only a few feet away from her. She had felt as though the entire audience must be aware of what had just happened between them, and that the blazing happiness he had ignited in her must be embarrassingly clear in her face.

But now all that was part of a past that was no longer relevant to her life, a past she'd thought she had blotted completely out of her mind.

'With my job I don't have time for all that sort of thing any more,' she said as dismissively as she could, her eyes on the uneven path. Perhaps she could steer him on to the present—in which they were strangers, and could take their leave of each other as soon as was decently possible. The sooner the better, as far as she was concerned.

'So what kind of college is this one you're involved in?' he asked, diverted by the change of subject.

'It's not in the least scholarly. At least, not for me. All I do is employ tutors and match them up with people who want to be taught things. It's a kind of agency and requires nothing but a bit of business sense.'

He picked up a pine cone, and lobbed it over the edge of the cliff only a few yards away from them. She found herself watching the muscles moving under the smooth, lightly tanned skin of his back. Every action spoke perfect physical control: no wasted energy, no unnecessary movement.

She remembered with sudden startling intimacy what it had been like to lie against that back in bed, and the salt taste of his skin when she'd put her lips to those powerful shoulders, or the contours of his spine.

He turned to look at her. 'Did you ever finish that business course you gave up?'

Her eyes flickered away from his, but she gave no other indication of the disconcerting trend her thoughts had just been taking. In the past she would have blushed fierily. Now it was much easier to hide things.

'A couple of years after we. . .split up—yes.'

He didn't comment on the choice of phrase. 'Split up' somehow suggested a mutual decision reached through discussion—very far from their own case. 'This business of yours,' he remarked after a pause. 'Another hidden talent?' Sarcasm again—it must be. They'd had rows about the way she'd spent money during that last year they were together.

She said nothing, but he continued undaunted. 'Do you have a school, or offices, or what?'

She took her time before answering, and managed to make her reply sound almost bored. 'It all works from home. I have a partner and we run the thing together. The students are taught either at their own houses, or they go to their tutors.'

'Sounds like easy money. Is it doing well?' He seemed genuinely interested.

Her reply was still cool. 'I wouldn't say it's easy money, but I've been lucky. My parents gave me the house, so I don't have to worry about rents or mortgages, business is quite good at the moment.'

There was a slight pause before he answered. 'Yes,' he said. 'There was always *mummy and daddy*.'

The undercurrent of bitterness was evident. She seemed to have got a genuine reaction out of him.

So it still rankled that she must have listened, in the end, to the voices of her parents, against the selfish all-absorbing claims of a man bent on personal success no matter what or whom he destroyed on his way. She wondered if any of his subsequent women—and she had no doubt that there'd been many—had found his ambition too much to take in the end.

'Your mother never approved of me, did she?' he was saying. 'A penniless north-country actor of unpretentious parentage as a son-in-law wasn't quite her cup of tea, was it?'

A son-in-law. Yes, it might have ended that way if. . . It was ironical that he could talk now in terms of a marriage. If only—but it was futile to think like that, she told herself firmly.

Her parents, ambitious for their only daughter, had always had a snobbish attitude towards Hal. From her mother's point of view, the son of a small-business man in a remote Yorkshire town would scarcely have made a suitable husband for the daughter of an extremely successful director of a company with offices in both London and Copenhagen.

Again, vivid memories blotted out the island scene before her, as she recalled the conversation she'd had with her mother the first time she'd brought Hal home—he'd faced a virtual inquisition across the dinner table the night before. Stephanie Hansen had been sitting in one of the elegant French drawing-room chairs. She always sat, and walked, like the fashion model she had once been. She was still beautiful, with a vivid, golden beauty that faded Nina's Scandinavian fairness, inherited from her father, to the paleness of a ghost beside her. Nina's 'colour', in those days, had come from her energy and inner fire.

'But Nina,' her mother had objected, 'acting is one of the most insecure jobs in the world. Even people with real talent often don't make it to the top. And he's just one of so many.'

'But Hal's fantastic on stage—he's *got* real talent!' she had defended him passionately; she'd never had any doubts even then that he would make it.

'Of course you think so.' The coolness in her tone had been intentionally damning. 'And I'm sure he's a very nice young man—but just don't get too involved with him, will you? You've got plenty of time, you're still so young.'

There was always a marked lack of enthusiasm in her mother's tone when she spoke about Hal after that, and Nina hadn't taken him home again for a while, preferring to visit her parents for occasional brief weekends alone. Somehow there was always a bright and good-looking young executive of her father's invited to dinner: competition for Hal. Her mother's unsubtle tactics had amused her, but when she next brought Hal for a weekend there had been a more serious attempt to dissuade her.

'I just wish you didn't spend so much time with him, Nina. His degree obviously doesn't matter to him, but you should be working at your course, not taking part in plays all the time.'

'That's not fair!' she had argued. 'Hal does care about his degree—but his acting's vital to him. The more he does while he's a student, the better chance he'll stand later. He's thinking of his future.'

'But I'd hate to see your future tied up with his.' Her mother had sounded almost angry. 'I think you made a mistake in moving into that flat with him. Hal's older than you. He should know what he's doing by now, and he can take all the risks he wants with his own career—but it's not fair to take risks with yours. I'm only thinking of you, darling.'

Nina had never found herself in conflict with her parents before. She had felt as though she were being torn in two.

'Hal means more to me than any stupid course!' she had said defiantly. 'I couldn't bear to lose him!'

She could still remember vividly how her mother had examined her faultless nail varnish while she'd sought the right words in this battle for her daughter's future. The 'right words', when she found them, hadn't weighed with Nina at the time, but she'd remembered them later.

'If you're worried about losing him already, Nina, then I'd think very carefully about what sort of commitment he has to you, if I were you. He's handsome and attractive, I'll grant you, but far too consciously charming for his own good. He could probably have any girl he wants—and don't think he doesn't know it!

And he isn't going to want to get tied down by anybody too early in what might turn out to be a very precarious career.'

Well, maybe events had proved her mother right about his lack of commitment to her. But looking back on it now, in all honesty Nina couldn't blame her failures as a student on Hal—neglecting her studies, and then giving up her course in favour of following him as he struggled to make a start in the theatre, had been her own responsibility. She had been old enough to know what she was doing with her time. . .

'So what does your mother think now?' Hal asked, his tone deliberately provocative.

His voice brought her abruptly out of her reverie. She should have been prepared for that question. The memory of her mother still choked her—it was something she couldn't talk about easily. Hal had caused such havoc in her life, there had never been time to heal the final breach between them.

'She died about three years ago,' she replied, with a finality that was intended to cut off any further lines of questioning in that direction.

'I'm sorry,' he said simply. 'I wouldn't have made those remarks if I'd known.'

She was surprised by the sudden change in his voice—he sounded genuinely concerned. She glanced across at him and found him looking at her, his expression thoughtful. She turned away, walking quickly, to hide the sudden overwhelming feeling of sadness that had come over her—it had all been such a waste. . .all that misguided love and unnecessary suffering.

She swallowed hard.

It was time to return to the attack and bring Hal under her fire for a change.

'Why haven't I seen your name on any of the blockbuster TV films or serials—or has it been up in lights all over the West End and I never noticed?'

If she had hoped to hear him on the defensive, she was disappointed. The deep voice merely sounded amused. 'You don't watch the right programmes. I've done quite a bit of television work, and toured a lot of the theatres. There were a couple of film parts too, but maybe they're not in the sort of thing you go to any more.'

'So when's the big break—or have you had it?' She hoped she didn't sound too sarcastic. A pretended lack of belief in his career was a very petty revenge to be taking for all those arrogant demands he had made on her in the past. But, if he had read her correctly, he didn't show it. There was still no more than amusement in his voice.

'It wasn't so much one big break as several smaller ones. Obviously a bit too small if they made so little impression! I did some work for the Royal Shakespeare Company a while ago, and I've been in the States since.'

She remembered reading about his success at Stratford, but she hadn't gone to see any of the plays.

They had to stop. Her foot had come out of the flip-flop and a stone had worked its way into the sole.

'You'd better go on,' she said quickly, seeing that this would make as good an excuse as any to part company. 'I'll only hold you up all the time. You're not staying at the harbour, are you? You probably want to get on much faster.'

He stood, hands on hips, watching the repairs. 'I'm in no hurry. Shall I do that?'

'No, thank you.' She pushed the thong back and was

trying to extract the sharp little stone with a small piece of stick.

'You'll make a hole in it and you won't have any shoe left.' He was looking at her, an amused expression in those unfathomable black eyes, that well-shaped mouth quirked into a smile she recognised. It was a glimpse of the old Hal, the Hal whose sheer physical presence in those early days had sent her pulse racing, and who had had only to touch her to turn her bones to water with the kind of desire she had never known before, and had never felt afterwards. His voice, when he spoke, had had that lovely deep tone she found irresistible.

As she walked on, very carefully to preserve what was left of her shoe, he strolled at her side. She was aware of every step he took beside her—of his disturbing masculine presence despite the indifference she'd thought she had acquired over the past few years, and of the apparently effortless charm he could exercise at will. It made her uncomfortably wary of him, and she was seeing too vividly, behind their polite, harmless exchanges, the world she had shut out of her life five years before.

At last they came to the descent to the harbour. A wide, shale-covered slope crossed the precipitous rock-fall of a dried-up mountain torrent, and narrowed into a winding goat track down the side of the hill. Automatically, Nina bent down to take off her shoes. It would be safer and easier to go down in bare feet.

'You go first,' she said dismissively. 'Don't wait for me. I'll take ages.' Shall I say goodbye now? she wondered. It would be a good moment to get rid of him.

There was a short, brittle pause while she waited for him to move. At five feet eight, she had never felt small, and in high heels could look many men in the eye, but Hal at over six feet had always made her feel insignificant. He now seemed to tower above her where he stood on the rise of the slope. With the wild Greek setting of the rocks and wind-tossed pines behind him, his strong gypsy-dark looks, and the turquoise in his ear, he could have been some Barbary pirate out of an old adventure story.

'There's a much easier solution than that,' he said, before she could nerve herself to start the formal leave-taking process. She was reminded again of that lithe professional agility as he sprang down, but, although she had read his intention before he reached her, just for an instant, and for a reason she didn't want to examine, she was unwilling to stop him.

But once he had put one arm round her back and the other under her knees and lifted her easily, she protested immediately.

'Don't be stupid, Hal! Put me down—you'll fall!' The annoyance in her tone belied the true nature of her feelings. She was finding the physical contact with him far more disturbing than she could ever have foreseen, and felt that she was under siege. If he had deliberately chosen his method of attack, he couldn't have done it better.

'You forget I'm practised at this sort of thing.'

'On stage, yes, but this isn't the place to try out your stunts!' It was a struggle to make the reply sound normal. He laughed, his lips disconcertingly close to her ear.

'There's nothing like getting in a sneak rehearsal.'

He seemed completely sure of himself as he picked his way down the rocks. She had one arm round his neck but, although she was genuinely apprehensive, pride wouldn't let her cling any closer. On her own, barefoot, she would have managed perfectly. This was taking an unnecessary risk, and she didn't want the contact with him that it forced on her.

His muscles were tensed, but she could feel no sense of undue strain in his body, and with his actor's technique he could make the whole exercise seem effortless. She was conscious of the feel of his bare back under her arm, of the smooth skin, and the muscles of his neck and shoulders. She could feel the even rise and fall of his ribs against her as he breathed, and the tickling contact of the dark hair on his chest against uncovered parts of her own skin. One hand rested lightly on her shirt under her breast as he held her. His skin smelled of suntan oil.

Once she had known every inch of that body as intimately as any woman could know a man, and he had known hers. Now they were virtual strangers—except that they had shared a past, and that could never be altered. What had been done could never be undone.

But, holding her as he was, for her he could be no gallant stranger rescuing a passing tourist by carrying her over the rocks. He was the first man she had ever loved, and her only lover.

'Put me down,' she said quietly. 'I'll walk from now on.' He set her down lightly, his hand lingering at her waist for perhaps seconds longer than necessary. She bent down to put on her flip-flops again, and he stepped back. They were almost at the goat track.

They descended to the harbour in silence, Nina all the way preparing the leave-taking speech she was going to make. She was no brilliant improviser like him, and preferred to have her lines well thought out in advance. But before she could turn to him to make the quietly dismissive little speech—What a surprise to see you. . . Hope your work goes well. . . I don't expect we shall meet again—he said, 'Have supper tonight with me at the taverna? I want to know all about the excitements of your life in Cambridge.'

'There aren't any.'

His lips twitched, but he didn't smile. 'Then I want you to know about the excitements of mine during company tours.'

Her reply was quick, and cold. 'You forget. I know only too well.'

She didn't want to be reminded of how, for more than a year after she had abandoned that business course against her parents' wishes, she had trailed round after him from one inadequate lodging to the next, always absorbed in his world, his concerns, his ambitions. She had had no real part in any of it, except to earn some of the money that kept them, but none of that had mattered until she had needed very suddenly, and very desperately, a well-paid job and an identity of her own.

She wasn't prepared for his next move. The gesture that had once been so familiar to her was now almost a physical shock. He took a step towards her and, putting his fingers lightly on her arms, ran his hands up and down in what was all but a caress.

'For old times' sake?'

The quiet depth in his voice, and the look in his eyes, could have been no more than an actor's technique. She knew it. And she hated herself, because even now, suspecting it for what it was, and knowing him as she did, she still wasn't able to resist it.

'All right,' she said ungraciously. 'I'll meet you at the taverna in an hour.'

CHAPTER TWO

For what old times' sake? she asked herself, as she showered the salt out of her hair ten minutes later. She was already regretting that inexplicable moment of weakness that had prompted her to accept Hal's invitation. You didn't have commemoration suppers, or whatever this was, to celebrate the untold misery someone had caused you. If you had any sense you got away as quickly as possible. This was a meeting that shouldn't have happened.

Perhaps he didn't remember the 'old times' the way she did. But she was aware that her memories had been distorted by something he had never known about; so perhaps whatever he had kept of their shared past could be looked back on with affection, or amusement, or that mild nostalgia when all the pain has slipped away and only the better bits remain.

There had, to be honest, been the better bits. At first. Although she now saw most of her career as coloured by Hal, her first year as a student had been wonderful. It had been very much an escape from ambitious and possessive parents, and, despite her enthusiastic involvement in the social activities which had taken up all her spare time, she had done quite well at the end of her first year of the course, fulfilling everyone's expectations of her. Then, in her second year, she had met Hal.

Their paths would never have crossed had it not been for their mutual interest in the stage. There were lots of student productions every term, and with friends at the university she had found herself included quite easily in their social world. But she had never expected to find herself in one of the star parts of *Romeo and Juliet*, and then to have gone with a surprisingly successful student tour round the major cities in England. She had thought then that it had been the best thing that had ever happened to her.

Older than the comparative teenagers in most of the university plays, Hal had had several advantages over his fellow undergraduates. He had already had some experience in theatre work, following an illness in his last year at school which had been the cause of his delayed entry into Oxford. Because of his obsession with the stage, it was with some reluctance that he had been persuaded to take up a university place at all. He had spent most of his three-year course in one play or another, and quickly became the best-known name in the student drama world.

Acting had been the passion of his life, and his academic studies hadn't featured very largely on his horizon. But despite his neglect of his work he had had the enviable ability to make the most of what he actually did, and to gain a very respectable degree—no one quite knew how. He had never been seen to open a book unless it had been a play-script.

Such a successful and powerful personality had not been without its effect on others and, of all those who came under Hal's irresistible spell, Nina supposed that she herself had been the most influenced by him—and not for her good, she now reflected sadly.

Her first and only lover, he had had an effect on her life that seemed in retrospect to have been totally destructive. Unless, of course, you could say that she had gained in the end by learning to acquire the rather cold, self-contained personality she could at times project to save herself, when necessary, from further harm.

Infuriating, self-centred, manipulative, using voice and body always so consciously to achieve the desired effects: that was the way she now saw him. And he had been able to hold her life in his hands in a way no other had done since. Such power carried with it serious responsibilities, and he had both ignored the responsibilities and abused the power.

Now, on a Greek island miles from either of their separate worlds, fate had suddenly brought them face to face again. But for what purpose? Was this an ending, a sort of badly produced final scene to a badly finished play, or was it the start of a whole new act, one she had never suspected existed? If so, she didn't want it. She could never go through that sort of pain again. She *would* never go through it—she was determined about that.

She had, after a painful struggle, sorted out her life at last. She had her own business, her house, her friends. She had something to aim at—financial success—and plenty of work to fill her time. There was a social life for her if she wanted it, although she had steered clear of any romantic involvements since Hal. 'Once bitten, twice shy!' she had reminded herself with a wry grin, on the couple of occasions when a friendship had seemed to be on the verge of something more.

That wasn't the whole answer, of course. She had a generous, loving nature, and although she wouldn't let herself brood on it she knew that there was a very important element missing from her life. But it was hard to find anything again that would match up to the best of what she had shared with Hal, and she wasn't prepared to settle for less. Different, perhaps, but not something that left her with the feeling that there was still so much missing.

Now, as she combed the tangles out of her wet hair, she tried to dismiss any serious thoughts about the past, and concentrate on the immediate problems of getting ready for supper at the taverna. There was no time to dry her hair, and she dressed quickly in a new pair of shorts and a shirt, tucking it into the waistband and rolling up the sleeves—the two garments were a matching vivid yellow; bright colours and black suited her. Usually, everything else made her look washed out, but she wished now that she had something white to show off her newly acquired tan—for once it wouldn't make her look like a ghost.

Just as well Hal and I never got married, she thought. A white wedding-dress would have been a disaster. But then, of course, there would have been no white wedding.

Although she had regretted her agreement to meet Hal from the moment she had given it, and was tempted not to turn up, by the time she set out for the taverna she was in a new and slightly reckless mood, induced, as she was well aware, by a couple of glasses of *raki* she had just drunk in the company of Yorgos and Katerina. They were her hosts at the small pension at which she had stayed on all her visits to the island so far. Katerina, a dark, slim woman in her thirties, had taken a liking to her guest of three summers, and, perhaps because Nina was careful never to intrude on the family's privacy despite the children's liking for her, often invited her to have an evening drink with them.

'This is a good drink, Nina!' Yorgos commented, refilling her glass. 'Very powerful, made from the skins of grapes.' He smiled under the greying moustache, his black eyes bright with humour. 'You will have a nice evening at the taverna! Perhaps meet some new tourist friends—who knows?'

She didn't think she'd mention the 'old' tourist friend she had just met. And anyway, after tonight she'd never be seeing him again.

By the time she got down to the harbour, she had drunk rather more than she had intended, and, by constantly reminding herself that whatever happened Hal was her past, not her future, had persuaded herself that one evening in his company couldn't make much difference one way or another—now she had got over the first shock of meeting him.

One thing she was sure of: she didn't want to go through several hours of those guarded exchanges they'd had on the way back from the beach. There were some things she wasn't going to talk about—things she would never discuss with anyone again—but she was prepared to put on an act. Not for the sake of old times, as Hal had suggested, but because—well, she wouldn't be seeing him again and she didn't want the memory of yet one more disastrous encounter to add to their past.

But despite her best resolutions, the evening didn't go according to plan. She might have known it, where Hal was concerned.

He was waiting for her, sitting under a tamarisk tree, sprawled back in his chair reading a paperback. There was a bottle of *retsina*—the characteristic resin-flavoured wine of Greece—on the table, and two glasses. His was half empty.

Even lounging as he was, he managed to look elegant. One hand was round the glass, the long, irregularly shaped fingers spread wide. He was wearing a white shirt open at the neck and a pair of respectable-looking jeans—she had expected to see him still in the old faded pair, half naked. The dark hair was evenly combed back, but the blue earring belied all signs of convention.

He looked up as she approached. 'Nina,' he said. 'You remind me of a nymph from the sea. You've even got wet hair to prove it.'

'And you look just like some medieval pirate!' she countered, feeling less sure of herself than she had only seconds before. He had always been too good at that sort of flirtatious personal sparring. 'Why on earth are you wearing that ridiculous earring?'

'So you don't think much of it?' His eyes met hers. There was the obvious question in them, but something else too, that she couldn't read.

'As a casual ornament—no, I don't. It's affected!' Again, attack was the best defence.

He laughed. 'You've become very conventional. . .or perhaps you always were underneath—just like your mother, and I never really noticed.'

That hurt. He hadn't wasted any time in renewing the hostilities of the afternoon.

Instantly, she found herself wanting to accuse him. There was a lot you never noticed about me! Perhaps I am like my mother in some things, but at least my mother listened when you didn't!

What was the matter with her? She shouldn't let him get to her—she had become quite good at keeping people at a distance when she needed to.

'Well?' she persisted. 'Why *are* you wearing it?'

If he had seen anything of her suppressed reaction to his last remark, he didn't show it.

'For a television play. They're all for authenticity. If

I wore a modern clip-on version it'd show in the close-ups. I can't say I wanted a hole in my ear, but now I've got the thing in I've got to keep it until I've finished filming.' He grinned. 'It has its amusing aspects—the looks I get going through passport controls, for example. So you think it's effeminate?'

There could be nothing effeminate, ever, about that powerfully built bearded male sitting opposite her! Their eyes met, her own unguarded for a second and full of humour.

'No,' she replied, smiling for the first time, 'that wasn't what I meant! You look far too much like a handsome corsair—you should have a cutlass in your teeth and be swinging from some rigging somewhere. . .' She hoped that he wouldn't pick up the compliment she had paid him in the middle of all that, and continued quickly, 'When do you start work on the television play?'

'As soon as I get back to England in another week. It's a historical effort in umpteen episodes about Elizabethan adventurers, so your pirate idea isn't too far wrong. Luckily I get killed off pretty quickly.' He paused. 'Then you don't think old age has been too unkind to me?'

She might have known he wouldn't let that comment pass. How old was he now—thirty? Thirty-one.

'Ask me in another ten years or so.' She made the remark without thought, and then could have kicked herself. This had to be an end—not another beginning.

He didn't let that one pass either. He asked slowly, 'Is that an admission that you might still want to know me?'

'Hal——'

'All right—you don't have to answer. Only I have to

tell you that I still find you as attractive as you ever were—more perhaps.'

She'd had her suspicions that they wouldn't get through the evening without crossing some dangerous ground, but how could it have happened so quickly? It seemed now that there was nothing that they could discuss safely. She didn't know what to reply without being rude and defensive—and that was a betrayal in itself.

But this time, to her relief, he didn't wait for her to say anything, but went back to their former neutral topic. 'I've got some theatre work starting when the TV serial finishes—a series of plays, including another Elizabethan one, so the beard and earring will come in useful a while longer.'

'You've got plenty of work, then?'

He gave something that sounded like a contemptuous snort. 'Oh, yes, I've got plenty of work—enough to last me years if I wanted to do it.' He put one long finger thoughtfully into his glass of *retsina*, and extracted a drowning fly. 'I'm not sure that I do.' He looked up, his dark eyes holding hers. 'But that's another story, and I don't think it's one you're prepared to listen to at the moment. So what shall I entertain you with—missed cues? Collapsing scenery? Disastrous sword fights?'

For a while, the encounter continued amicably. Hal ordered more wine, and food—a variety of Greek dishes, with swordfish steaks, grilled with herbs and garnished with huge slices of lemon.

It was a pity, she thought, as she listened to the gossip of the acting world, that they couldn't just be the chance-met strangers she had tried to imagine earlier—she could have let herself like him, and respond to him without the need to be cautious. He was a good story-teller, and took her interest for granted, notwithstanding her earlier remarks that day. As always, she was held despite herself just by the power of his voice, but later she found it disturbing to discover that she could remember virtually nothing of what he had said—she had been far more interested in his physical presence.

She had watched the gestures of his long-fingered hands as he explained the construction of a set—essential to the understanding of some unlikely comic tale—and the changing expressions in his dark eyes as he told the anecdotes. In the dusk, by the taverna lights, he looked more deeply tanned, and his teeth were white in the dark-bearded face when he smiled.

It was some time later when she said, 'I got the impression you weren't staying at the harbour?' There was something she wanted to make sure of.

'I wasn't—last week. I've been down here for the last couple of nights. You never asked.'

'So we might have met at any time in the last two days?'

He surveyed her impassively, the black eyes enigmatic. 'We might,' he said, 'but we didn't.'

'And why was that, I wonder?' There was no way he could take the question as innocent speculation—she was looking him straight in the eyes and he must know that what she was really telling him was that he had deliberately avoided her, until that meeting on the beach.

He said nothing. By now, with the *retsina* and the *raki* she had drunk with Katerina and Yorgos, she had had more alcohol than she was used to, and she had forgotten to be cautious. 'What made you finally decide to say hello to me today? Or was it the sight of my nudity that overcame your better judgement?' She couldn't help the sarcasm that tinged the last remark, and she wasn't surprised when he reacted to it.

'You know, Nina,' the deep voice was casually conversational, and gave no hint of what was coming, 'you've changed a lot. You've become quite nasty over the years, even if you have grown more beautiful. For some reason I've yet to fathom, you're sarcastic and defensive and bitter underneath all that polite social manner. Don't think I've been sitting here for the best part of an hour without noticing that you've let me do all the talking, as long as it's been about nothing that really mattered to either of us. And nearly every time I ask you something your eyes go blank—as though little shutters have come down over them—while you think up what sort of an answer you're going to give me. Have some more *retsina*.'

She was shocked at the unexpected directness of his attack. She hadn't really meant it to go like this at all.

'Well, had you seen me before this afternoon?' she persisted, openly resentful now and determined that if, underneath it all, he had only set up this meeting to get his own back in some way, she wasn't going to stay around much longer to let it happen.

'Yes. Last night and the night before.'

'And you recognised me?'

'I told you I've never forgotten those eyes. I watched you both nights. I've got a room here, above the taverna. You eat early, and I eat late.'

She stared at him across the table in a tense and hostile silence. So that whole episode earlier on the beach had been carefully staged. He had waited for her to come out of the sea having known for two days who she was, just as she had suspected. He had probably planned exactly what he was going to do, and say, and had wanted to catch her at a disadvantage.

So what was the point of prolonging this whole charade? He was only trying to make a fool of her. She had just one more day to get through on the island, and she could easily avoid him if she chose to. He hadn't really changed one bit! Angrily, she got to her feet.

'Hal—there's no point in this——' she began, but before she had got any further his hand had shot out and clamped itself on her arm.

'Sit down. There's no need to react like that.'

Of course, whatever she did, he would be able to make it look as though she was the one creating a scene. Her eyes met his angrily, and then she realised that there was no point either in fighting—even now she would be no match for him.

She was beginning to feel the first stirrings of a cold, secret fear that everything she had believed dead was in fact still there, deeply buried inside her, so that what she had hoped was a genuine indifference to him was really only a fragile outer shell, an inadequate armour that he had already found a way to pierce. She had believed that emotions and desires could be killed, if not by someone else, then by you, yourself. You could stifle them, so that in the end they were no longer there. But he had already disturbed her too much for that to be true.

She no longer knew what she felt for him, but there was no way that they could avoid the past. It overshadowed everything they said, and all those unspoken questions lay behind every casual enquiry. She shouldn't have had so much to drink—she needed all her wits about her to handle something like this.

'What do you want to get out of this, Hal?' she asked after a pause. She was more in control of her voice now—she managed to sound calm, almost expressionless.

'Something to fill a gap in my existence, perhaps?' It wasn't the kind of answer she had expected. He went on, 'This is a beautiful island. It has a sense of reality, and a sort of quiet purpose that makes one realise that most of us live crazy lives. It makes an actor's life seem the craziest of the lot.'

He sounded perfectly serious, and, coupled with his earlier remark, the comment prompted her to ask, 'Does that mean you're beginning to discover the stage scenery's only made of paint and canvas?'

Again there was a hint of sarcasm in her tone, but as long as he wasn't attacking her she was prepared to carry on the discussion. And she didn't have to explain what she meant—he understood immediately. In the past, that had been one of the most exciting aspects of their relationship. Often it had been as though they shared the same thought processes.

He smiled at her in the way that had used to make her heart turn over. 'In a manner of speaking.' His voice was deep and quiet. 'But that doesn't mean there's anything wrong with the paint and canvas. I've always known about the limitations. . .perhaps it's just that I can't so easily accept them any longer.'

She was surprised. This was something different from the old Hal. If she hadn't been so wary, the note of regret in that disturbing voice would have prompted a sympathetic response—with anyone but him she could have shown concern.

Don't let him involve you, she told herself firmly. You won't have to see him again. If you can't remain detached, it's better not to be involved at all.

They got up from the table then. It was late, and had long been dark, a red moon rising out of the sea to hang like a bright disc above the slowly turning sails of a windmill on the cliff-top.

She began to prepare a little leaving speech but, before she could make up her mind to say it, he took her by the elbow. It was just as though an electric current had suddenly passed down her arm. It needed all her self-control not to pull away instantly. She didn't want him touching her—she was far too aware of him for her own comfort—but she didn't want to signal it to him so obviously. He would probably take advantage of it.

'Come down on the beach for a while. I want to talk to you.'

'You've been talking all evening. It's late. Is there anything left to say?' Her tone was not encouraging.

'We haven't been talking at all—just making social noises. I hardly know anything about you—not any more. You've been just an audience all evening, and I get enough of those. Tell me something—anything! Do you still like eating sticky cakes at midnight?'

She turned to glance at him where they stood, a few feet from the lights of the taverna. His eyes glittered in the half-light and he was smiling. But they were on dangerous ground again. He was trying to get her to break down the barriers he had known were behind the whole of their conversation.

She shrugged. 'I can't say it's something I think about very often!' That was true, and she didn't want to remember it now.

He chuckled and she felt his hand on the small of her back. The slight pressure told her to walk, and she stepped quickly forward to escape his touch.

'I could never understand how you ate so much and stayed so thin.'

'You were thin yourself,' she retorted, but she didn't

like the personal reminiscence. He was determined to lead them still further away from the safe, boring topics of the present that couldn't disturb either of them.

'Yes, but I didn't get out of bed every night to eat my way through half a chocolate cake.'

She didn't reply. She had a vision of herself sitting on the end of their bed, trying to talk and eat a piece of cake at the same time, dressed in Hal's towelling bathrobe. The crumbs kept falling down her front. Hal—a thinner, beardless Hal—was lying in bed laughing at her. Afterwards, he had pretended to lick them off her, and they had both laughed.

They walked slowly along the beach, towards the far cliff path that would take them up to the windmill. She had walked there the night before, alone and undisturbed, enjoying the bland peace of the moonlight. Now she saw that it wasn't just the calm of the night she had been appreciating, but the hard-won calm of her own even, ordered life. She didn't want it disturbed; and most of all she didn't want it disturbed by this man.

She had known it was a mistake to give in to his request; she wanted this meeting over as quickly as possible—ended, neatly and finally, once and for all. This walk on the beach was artificially prolonging it. Tonight *must* be an end, not the opening of another act.

Again she was aware of every movement of Hal beside her. His height dominated her, and he walked more slowly than she, his long legs seeming incapable of fitting their stride to hers. There was something about his sheer proximity, something that she had deliberately banished from her mind, but recognised as that indefinable pull of attraction that had always been between them.

What was he doing with her now, she wondered? What motive could he have for seeking out her company? She had made it embarrassingly clear that she didn't welcome his attention, and that she was reluctant to talk. They might have had supper together for the sake of their former relationship, but she had tried to make certain that they wouldn't speak of 'old times'. His allusion to the midnight cakes had been the only one specifically connected with that topic.

He stopped walking suddenly, and she stood, about two feet away from him, and asked, 'Shall we go back?'

'I was just going to ask you about Cambridge,' he said. 'Who is this partner of yours? Anyone I used to know?'

She watched the dark movement of the sea, and the small fishing boats rocking gently against their moorings. 'No,' she said, reluctantly. She wanted to give him as little information as possible, but felt obliged to add, 'He's a friend, but someone I met since I knew you.'

'Does he live with you?'

The question, so casually dropped, annoyed her. It was none of his business! She was tempted to lie, to warn him off finally in case he saw himself in a new role—meeting a former lover on a romantic island by moonlight. There were too many plays which had that sort of background to the plot! Perhaps she should tell him that she lived with Ed. He'd never find out the truth, so what did it matter?

'I don't see that it's any concern of yours,' she replied coldly, ducking out of the lie. She might save it up until later.

He started walking again, and reluctantly she walked beside him. She would tell him she was going back to her room. He had no business to be interrogating her. He had given up his right to ask anything of her years ago. She took a deep breath and then, as she glanced sideways at him, saw him watching her.

'It isn't my business,' he said quietly. 'But I wasn't asking about your sex life. I was just wondering what arrangements you had about your house and your tutorial establishment, and whether the whole thing ran economically for you and your partner, whoever he is.' A note of humour crept into the deep voice. 'Now I will ask about your sex life. What are you doing alone on this island? Haven't you got a husband or lover to keep you in order that you have to wander about at night with disreputable actors like me?'

'I thought you were trying to impress me earlier with how very reputable you had become!' She evaded his question.

'It was merely a figure of speech. Well?' He wasn't going to be put off.

'I could ask the same of you.'

'All right. I'll tell you, since I seem to have less to hide in my life than you have in yours. Although there have been one or two women since you, as you might have guessed—actors aren't renowned for celibacy—there isn't one at the moment, and there hasn't been for some time. The last was a disaster for various histrionic reasons. So, I am free to come to this as yet unspoilt, unfrequented island to sort out a few little confusions in my existence, before I take up such commitments as I have back home.'

'What confusions?'

'Ah. That's not fair!' he said quickly. 'It's your turn now. What are you hiding? If you've transformed your respectable parent-donated dwelling into a brothel, I shan't turn a hair. Or tell the police and have you raided.'

He almost got a smile out of her, and she softened a little. 'My dwelling remains perfectly respectable, thank you, and there's nothing much to say about it. I don't live with Ed, nor he with me. He's a friend and a business partner, and he lives with his wife Jenny who's an accountant and also a friend. She does our books for us, all strictly above board. So there's nothing to tell the police or anyone else about.'

'How do you spend your time when you're not making inspired marriages between would-be scholars and their pedants?'

'That's a very pompous way to put it!'

'It sounds like a pompous job! So. . .?'

'Coming to Greece, like now.'

He laughed. 'That's not quite what I meant. You must have the odd weekend, afternoon, evening. . .what do you do? Write? Paint? Go to evening classes in tatting? Pick up men in discos? What?'

She tempted to give in to this renewed, lighter mood in the conversation, but, after everything else that had been said, it was too dangerous. She stopped walking and turned to him.

'Hal, what's the point of this?' she asked edgily. 'We've been out of each other's lives for a long time now. We won't meet again. Don't you think it would be better just to forget about the past and leave the present alone? We don't know each other any longer.'

He stood, hands in pockets, lounging with a casual animal grace. He looked completely relaxed, while there was an underlying tension in her that felt as though it might twist her shoulders, her neck, and the whole of her spine into knots. She felt threatened by him, dominated by his height, his attitude, his sheer male presence.

'That's not true. We do know each other—a whole lot more than any other chance-met tourists on this island. But I've found out less about you than I would about any stranger I might talk to. . . And there is a point to all this, even if you don't see it. I don't like untidy endings, and what I discovered today was that for me there never really has been an ending. You left everything hanging in the air—no explanations, nothing. I'd like to know why. Just to set the record straight, if nothing else.'

'You never bothered to find out before, when it mattered!' she flashed at him, betrayed suddenly into verbal violence by the threat he posed. They had been on a knife-edge of some sort of outburst all evening—it seemed inevitable now that it all had to end this way. 'Why do you have to rake it all up again now?' she went on angrily—she was letting her emotions take a dangerous hold of her. 'We're not in one of your damn plays, Hal! Life isn't like art—or haven't you found that out yet? There's no neat knitting up of the plot at the end—happy-ever-after marriages, and people re-united with long-lost children and. . .oh, *hell*——' Her voice broke on something like a sob.

The hand she put up to hide her face was shaking and she quickly withdrew it. She had known his instinct would be to reach out and touch her, to try to comfort her for whatever unexplained grief it was he must surely have seen seconds before—she had to get away! She couldn't risk any more questions.

She was speaking. 'I've got a splitting headache. I'm going back to my room. Thank you for supper, Hal.' She had already turned to go. 'Goodbye.'

'Nina——'

There were several yards between them now. She was walking fast, almost running, her hair flapping silver in the moonlight. It wouldn't do him any good to pursue her—she was determined to let nothing happen between them again, not even a casual passing friendliness.

CHAPTER THREE

'YOU will let me dry it?' Elli demanded, as Nina, twisting a pale rope of dripping hair on top of her head, groped for the towel.

Elli's hairdressing efforts were a long-established ritual between them. The lively little nine-year-old Greek was fascinated by the silver fairness of her tourist guest's hair, so different from her own dark curls, and brushed and combed and plaited and curled—the latter with a depressing lack of success—and chatted away in erratic English while Nina sat with a book she had no hope of reading.

Nina was making very leisurely preparations for the ferry. There were hours and hours yet to while away before it arrived. It was scheduled to appear at ten, but experience had taught her that there would be no sign until well after midnight. She still had to pack, but that wouldn't take more than ten minutes; she had brought minimal holiday clothing and only one soft bag to carry things.

With her head swathed in a towel, she stepped out into the little courtyard of the villa. The light was already fading, making the whitewashed walls bright in the gloom. Pots of green basil stood by the wrought-iron gates and along the tops of the enclosing walls, and someone in a nearby house had a radio on, playing typical Greek bouzouki music. It had all become very familiar to her. She would miss the peaceful, easy way of life, and the friendly islanders.

Katerina had asked earlier that evening if she would

eat with them, and she had accepted with enthusiasm: it wasn't just that she enjoyed their company—it was also an excellent way of avoiding Hal, something that she hadn't succeeded in doing earlier that day, despite her best efforts.

Elli fetched a chair from the kitchen, and a small stool on which to put her hairdressing equipment. The courtyard was her salon, and Nina was quite happy to enter into the spirit of the game to please her, sitting where she was told and having long discussions about possible styles. Then Elli seized the comb, and began to tease out the long damp strands.

'You are eating with us tonight? It is so sad that you have to go. When will you come back? You could come in April—we have rooms for guests then.'

'Ouch. I have to work in April. I'll come back next summer—for longer. I promise.'

There was a few seconds' pause while Elli concentrated on a tangle, and then she demanded, 'Who is that man today? I and Katia walked with our friends in the afternoon and you were with a man on the beach near the olive trees.'

'Oh, was I?' This wasn't a good start! She wasn't even prepared to think about Hal, let alone be questioned about him. Her third encounter with him had been both unexpected—because she had taken care to avoid yesterday's haunts—and humiliating. 'So what were you doing hanging about in the olive trees?' she demanded, in mock disapproval.

'What is "hanging about"?'

'It means being there with nothing to do!'

Elli laughed. 'But we have something to do—watching you! But you were with the man, so it was not good to come down. You went swimming and had a race with him.'

If that was what it looked like to Elli, well and good!

'He is your boyfriend?'

'No. Just a tourist I met.' Rather a casual way to dismiss such a cataclysmic interview with Hal, she thought wryly. He had forced information out of her she didn't want to give, succeeded in making her cry—which was something she hadn't done for years—and, without appearing to be aware of it, challenged her to reassess their entire relationship.

She had been sunbathing on an unfrequented beach below the olive groves. It wasn't one she liked, and she'd only chosen it to avoid Hal.

A disturbed night, followed by an enforced sunbathe on her least favourite beach on her last day on the island, hadn't put her in a very good frame of mind. She'd tried to read, but there had been an irritating breeze, and she'd ended up with the book over her face.

She hadn't known how much time had passed in a sun-drugged haze when she had heard the crunch of pebbles behind her head. Glancing upwards from under the pages of her paperback, she'd found Hal looking down at her. He had been standing with his feet just behind her head, and he had seemed to obscure the sky—dark skin, dark beard, dark eyes. A shadowing of curled hair had darkened his chest. The gold had glittered in his ear and the turquoise had hung brilliant against the black hair. She might have known he wouldn't leave her alone.

'What are you doing here?' she'd demanded coldly.

The corners of his mouth had twitched, but hadn't smiled. 'A cat may look at a queen.'

'Go away. There are lots of beaches on this island. Why did you have to choose this one? It's not even very nice.'

The dark eyes had narrowed to dangerous slits. 'I'm not choosing the beach. I'm choosing you.'

It had been no use getting angry. She couldn't win a fight with him standing over her like that. But he hadn't broken her outward composure yet—cold indifference would work in the end. He would grow bored and leave her.

'Go away and look for the goats you said you wanted for company. We said goodbye yesterday. I'm catching the ferry tonight.'

She had slid the book up over her face again, as a gesture of finality.

'Good. That leaves us about ten hours.'

'What's that supposed to mean?'

'That we've got plenty of time to renew our acquaintance.'

Nina had bitten her lip, and had rolled over on to her stomach so that he couldn't look directly at her face.

'I thought I made it clear yesterday that as far as I'm concerned, there's no acquaintance to renew,' she had said in tones as ice-clear as she could make them. 'Would you move, please? You're standing where I want to put my book.' And she had stared pointedly at the light-coloured espadrilles and the frayed ends of his jeans.

After that, things had gone from bad to worse. Looking back on it now, as Elli's light fingers played with her hair, she could see that what she had at first dismissed as a childish desire on Hal's part to provoke her had in fact been part of a carefully orchestrated plan.

First he irritated her beyond endurance, taunting her with her unconvincing attempts to read. Then, having driven her to take refuge in the sea, he followed her in and chased her, exhausting her in her efforts to evade contact with him in an environment which allowed him to tease her, and even touch her, in games she couldn't fight off—she could neither argue effectively, nor ignore him.

Finally, when she swam slowly back to the beach, chilled and utterly drained of energy, to flop face down on her towel, he launched his real attack—just when she was least expecting it.

He stretched out on the pebbles a couple of feet away from her, lying on his side, watching her, his dark head supported on one outflung arm. With the earring still vivid against the wet, black hair, he looked more like an Elizabethan adventurer than ever.

Exhaustion deceived her into thinking that they had established a sort of truce, and she was about to make some comment on his appearance.

But there was no way that she could have foreseen the question he asked her, before she could even open her mouth. With one bound he leapt every one of the invisible barriers straight into the subject they had so carefully avoided all through those edgy exchanges they had had the night before.

'Why didn't you answer my letters?'

Letters? What letters? Her heart nearly missed a beat. She had never received anything from him! If he *had* written, then. . . She licked her lips. Her mouth was dry. 'Hal——' Her voice sounded hoarse. 'Don't. . .' But she no longer had the energy or the will to fight.

'Don't what? Ask you to explain why you walked out on me all of a sudden one day and never came back? Or why you wouldn't speak to me on the phone? Or why you never acknowledged a single one of my letters—did you even *read* them?'

She lay perfectly still. Suddenly, she couldn't

answer. What he had just said could change her whole view of him. For years she'd been telling herself that he'd just let her go, without a word, because her bitterness had somehow made the separation easier to bear. But now it seemed that it hadn't been like that at all.

But she didn't want to know any more—it was too late to change anything. He was only making it all so much worse to remember. 'It doesn't matter now,' she said desperately. 'It's all in the past. Why can't we just forget it? We won't see each other after today.'

Her face was giving too much away, she was sure of it. She rested her forehead on her arms to hide whatever it was her expression would tell him. She didn't want to think about the implications of what he had said just yet.

'There's no guarantee that we won't meet again,' he said. His tone was empty of any expression. 'Don't you think you owe me an explanation at least? I've had to wait over five years for it.'

'Don't pretend you cared about me all that time, because I won't believe it!' Her bitter reply was purely defensive. It had been so much easier to believe that he hadn't really loved her.

'I cared enough not to forget you. I cared enough to recognise you the second I saw you over five years later.'

She drew a shuddering breath, and tried to control her thoughts. What sort of revenge was he trying to get, anyway—humiliation? And all the talk of caring—what did it amount to? Maybe he had written to her afterwards, but if he'd really cared he'd have done something to stop her leaving him: all the signs had been there, for weeks and weeks. He had been too caught up in his own selfish concerns to notice. He hadn't stopped to listen, even when——

'Well?' he prompted. 'If it was so long ago and none of it matters, as you keep saying, why can't you tell me? I'd like to know—just for the record, as I told you. Why didn't you answer the letters?'

'I never got any.' She could scarcely speak.

There was an infinitesimal pause, and he said, 'Is that true?'

'Of course it's true. . .' Her words were muffled. 'Why would I bother to lie after all this time?'

'I wrote six or seven times.'

She was silent, shocked by the implications. It was hard to accept that her mother had had such an active part in separating them. Then she asked, 'Why did you write?' She knew the answer, but she couldn't stop herself asking.

'Surely that's obvious?' For the first time there was a roughened edge to that liquid voice. 'Was it too much to ask for an explanation even then? One day you were there. The next you were gone—no note, nothing. Don't you think I might have wondered what it was I'd done? Or maybe even *not* done? I tried to see you twice, but I might have known that that would be a waste of time——'

'Where?' she interrupted him. 'Where did you try to see me?'

'At your parents', of course. Your mother was doing her guard-dog act.'

She kept her face resolutely hidden—all that unhappiness! And it need not have happened the way it did at all. . . She could hardly bear to think about it—the only consolation lay in the fact that he had never known the real reason she had gone to her parents, so in the end the letters wouldn't have made any difference. . .

'Tell me, were all those dismissive messages really from you? What did you do, give her a briefing every day in case I called?' The edge had taken on a recognisable bitterness, and she was stung into a reply.

'I didn't give her any messages—I wasn't there!'

'Then where were you?' he demanded.

She didn't dare to look at him now; it was hard enough just to control her voice. When she spoke at last, it was an evasion. He held the key, but she wasn't going to show him how to turn the lock.

She began hesitantly, her face buried in her arms. 'I tried to tell you, Hal. . .I tried to talk to you lots of times. But you weren't interested. You were too obsessed with your career. . .and even when I wanted to tell you something important, you didn't really listen. At least my parents cared—they made mistakes, but they wanted what they believed was best for me. You didn't. You were only interested in what was best for yourself——' She broke off. If he had been trying to humiliate her, he had succeeded. If she said any more, he would know she was crying. She heard him move abruptly on the stones beside her, as though to deny what she had just said, but he couldn't.

There was a long pause.

'So you went home. Don't you think you might have left a note?' He sounded angry, but she made no reply. 'Damn it, Nina, was it so bloody difficult to have told me you were going to your parents?'

Memory was a strangely selective thing—she *had* told him. They'd even had a row about her spending the train fare to go all the way down to Sussex just when he had an important audition. He wanted her with him, and they couldn't afford to spend any more money. . . It was unbearable to think about it now.

And it was hard to accept the thought of those letters—he hadn't been as unfeeling as she had believed, but it was too late to change anything. They didn't alter the reasons she had made the original decision.

The silence between them lengthened into minutes. Eventually she sat up, brushing her hair back quickly in a gesture that drew the side of one arm across her face. It took all trace of the tears with it, as she had intended.

She knew now the way to defeat him: while she remained silent, unresponsive, there was nothing he could do—no way he could torture her with all those things best left buried in the past. There was no way she was going to let them—or him—ruin her future too. . .

As she thought about it now, in the calm dusk of Katerina's courtyard, she saw how she had made her first mistake in allowing his teasing to goad her into showing her irritation. His subsequent tactics had further broken down her control, and she couldn't afford to lose more ground to him. There were still barriers he hadn't even guessed at. She wasn't going to let him try.

She couldn't help dwelling on the way in which her parents had forced her into a position of choice: Hal or them. She had been torn for a while between the two, but in the end it had been her parents who had shown love and concern when she'd needed it; Hal had had his chance, and he hadn't even listened. His own concerns had come first, as they always had. But her parents had made her pay a price, and she was only now beginning to discover the full cost of her decision.

Her mother had died believing that Nina still hated her for forcing that choice, and after her death Nina's father had returned to his native Denmark where she had seen him very rarely since. When their large Queen Anne house in Sussex had been sold, the loss of her childhood home had been a blow to her; most of her associations with it had been happy ones—although Hal had hated that house. To him it had symbolised everything in her mother's attitudes that had been unacceptable to him.

From the day she had met Hal there had been neither peace nor tranquillity in her life. He had caused strife in her family, and his relationship with her had swung from one dramatic extreme to the other. It was strange to remember now that at first she had thrived on it.

Afterwards, when his absence had created an aching void that nothing could fill, she had made a new life and found new friends, without ever really losing the pain he had caused her. She had learned to live with it by shutting off part of herself, but she would never dare again to open those doors of her own free will. Nor was she going to allow Hal to force them.

She hadn't let him see the tears on her face, and she hadn't given him an answer. He had left soon after that, with a comment about seeing her at supper, and she had made up her mind to stay at the villa for the rest of the day, avoiding him until she was safely on the ferry.

Her thoughts now were broken by the eruption on the scene of Dimitri: thirteen, skinny, and as lively as his sister Elli.

'You are playing with me now, Nina! You said—you

promised—yesterday!' Dark eyes sparkling, and out of breath from a run up the street, he thrust himself between his sister and their guest, upsetting the 'salon' table and Elli in one go. Elli broke into a spate of tearful Greek, and Dimitri, arguing vehemently, called his mother from the kitchen to intervene on his behalf. Katerina, wiping floury hands on her apron, emerged briefly to speak with unmistakable sharpness to both of them.

Despite the row, Nina was amused. She liked both children, and was long accustomed to their arguments. Then she caught Katerina's eye, and the two women smiled at each other.

'OK, you two!' she said decisively. 'We can easily do both things if we sit at the table. Elli can comb my hair while I play backgammon.'

Ellie's agreement was reluctant—she no longer had sole claim to Nina's attention—but she moved the chair to the table while Dimitri ran to fetch the board.

Relative peace then ensued while Dimitri and Nina, engrossed in the game, struggled to outwit each other, and Elli amused herself plaiting and unplaiting Nina's hair. The contest over the backgammon was an old one—Dimitri had kept the scores from the previous holiday, and Nina had found herself sitting down to the same life-and-death struggle even on the first night of her return.

They switched on the courtyard light when it began to grow dark, Dimitri appreciatively sniffing the delicious smells of cooking emanating from the kitchen. Then Katerina came out with a glass of wine for Nina. They were waiting for the return of Yorgos from the shop he kept by the harbour, before they set the table.

'You must drink lots of wine, Nina!' Dimitri encouraged. 'It's good for your brain. You must take more chances!'

Nina, the dice in her hand, caught the mischievous look in his eye and laughed. Her hair, teased out by the ministrations of Elli, floated round her shoulders, and her loose white shirt and cotton jeans were bright in the lights of the courtyard.

And that was how Hal saw her—bright, laughing, completely caught up in the game and the children. There was almost a softness about her, and an indefinable quality that had not appeared at their other meetings—a glimpse of the past.

Nina looked up suddenly, and felt her heart miss a beat. She had been expecting Yorgos, but the tall, bearded man in the gateway was nothing like the stocky Greek. In an instant her face changed.

At that moment Katerina came out of the kitchen, with a plastic bread basket in her hands.

'I was looking for Nina,' Hal explained. He was completely relaxed, hands in the pockets of his faded denims. He was smiling. 'I thought we might be having supper together.'

Katerina glanced quickly from one to the other, misinterpreting the look on Nina's face. 'You are Nina's friend from the beach? Yes, Elli told me. I am so sorry—I asked Nina to have supper with us tonight before she goes. I did not know you had arranged this.'

'No, it's all right, really,' Nina interrupted hastily. 'There was no arrangement.' She avoided Hal's eye.

'You are leaving together tonight?'

'No,' said Hal. 'But I was hoping I might see Nina before she catches the ferry.' Damn him, and that actor's voice! He knew exactly the right intonations to sound like regret and polite withdrawal at the same time, when he meant nothing of the sort.

Of course, he was warmly invited to stay for supper. Nina gave him a deliberately hostile look. He met her eyes fully, and then turned shamelessly to Katerina and held out his hand with a smile. 'My name's Hal,' he said. 'Thank you for the invitation. I should very much like to stay, if it isn't inconvenient.'

Katerina returned his smile. 'You are very welcome. We are waiting for my husband before we begin to eat, but perhaps you would like some wine now? Dimitri.' There was a loud protest in Greek, which caused Katerina some amusement. 'He plays Nina for the honour of Greece!' she exclaimed, and went to fetch the wine herself.

Nina, acutely conscious of Hal's presence, said nothing and concentrated ferociously on the game.

'You should have told me you already had an arrangement for supper,' he said. He must have guessed she hadn't; she would have produced it as the perfect excuse to avoid meeting him.

Elli had given up on her hair for the time being, and was bringing a third chair for Hal. He turned the chair round and sat astride it, resting his arms along the back to watch the game. 'You are the family backgammon champion, are you?' he asked Dimitri, with a grin.

Dimitri grinned back. 'Of course,' he announced nonchalantly. 'I beat my father. You play this game? Play with me?'

Hal winked at Elli. 'I only play professionals, so I'll wait to see how you do against Nina before I tell you.'

Elli giggled, and squirmed her way into Nina's lap. 'Play with Dimitri!' she pleaded. 'You must beat him—Nina never wins!'

Nina was aware that Hal was looking at her, but she didn't meet his eye.

'Ah,' he said, 'that's because she doesn't have the right strategy. How long has she been playing this game?' Outwardly he was conducting his conversation entirely with the children, who were already fascinated by him.

'I teach her two years before.'

'Then you have an unfair advantage—all your years of experience. I'll play on Nina's side, and you see if you can beat the two of us.'

'And I'll play for Nina also!' Elli announced.

When Dimitri protested, Hal said cunningly, 'Just think of the victory if you win—three against one! You'll be the hero of the village.'

Nina wasn't sure why Hal was involving himself in the game. It certainly gave him an excuse to involve himself with her, but his enjoyment seemed genuine. She was surprised—this easy rapport with children was something she had never seen in him before. There was an irony in it she didn't want to think about. But maybe the whole thing was just good acting.

Elli was lying against her. Nina rested her chin on the curly dark head and said, 'Perhaps it would be better if the two of you continued the game. I'll watch.'

'Why?' Hal challenged, forcing her to meet his eyes. 'Afraid of getting too involved? Or is it the thought of playing on the same side as me that puts you off?'

She knew that he intended her to take the words at more than their obvious meaning. 'Hal——!' she said warningly. It wasn't fair to use the children.

During the game that followed, she was too distracted by Hal to pay much attention to what she was doing. She let him take the dice from her fingers, horribly aware of the moment when their hands touched, and then watched him join forces with Elli. The two of them, with unholy glee, set out to block all Dimitri's moves.

By the time Yorgos returned from the village there was a very noisy battle going on. Hal had decided that

England's honour was at stake, while Nina, her attention very pointedly fixed on the young Greeks, sipped her wine and encouraged both sides in turn.

Introductions interrupted play for a while, and she used Yorgos' arrival to withdraw from the game and help Katerina to set the meal out. There was some argument over table space, and supper had to wait while the game was finished. Dimitri won, and demanded everyone's attention, but Nina, waiting to put down a bowl of olives and following the final stages of play from behind Hal's chair, had seen the last moves.

'You let him get away with that, didn't you?' she asked Hal, her voice pitched too low to be heard over the jubilant exclamations of Dimitri.

He looked up at her, one corner of his mouth curling into a smile. 'What you call a strategic defeat—it didn't look as though anyone was going to get any supper!' Then, before she had a chance to move away, he reached out and pulled her against him. She almost dropped the bowl of olives, and her body tensed instantly. 'That was your first completely spontaneous remark of the evening. Progress?'

She couldn't pretend she didn't know what he meant, and she couldn't make a scene. She intended her smile to be no more than a polite one, but somehow she caught the amusement in Hal's eyes, and it turned genuine instead. His fingers tightened momentarily on her arm, and the smile faded.

'Do you think we could move the board off the table now to make room for the food?' she said coolly.

'I'll do it!' Dimitri offered. 'Play again after, Hal?' Hal laughed, and released her. 'Maybe tomorrow, if you come down to the café—I'll have nothing to do once Nina's gone.'

'Nina is your girlfriend?' Dimitri enquired, with far too much interest.

'She used to be.' She had stepped quickly away from him, but she knew he was looking at her. 'Perhaps she will be again. Who knows?'

'Ah, lovers' quarrels!' Yorgos said indulgently, his moustache spread in a knowing grin. 'Women are the devil, Hal—they never know what they want. You have to let her know who is the boss!'

Hal laughed, that deep golden laugh of genuine amusement.

'You know, Yorgos, I just might!'

Nina, angry and embarrassed, retreated instantly into the kitchen. He had found a new way of provoking her, and was deriving quite a lot of enjoyment out of it.

'You have been to this island before, Hal?' Katerina asked when they had sat down to supper, Nina next to Yorgos at the head of the table and only diagonally opposite Hal.

'It's my first visit—I've never been to Greece before.'

'You like it?'

'It's beautiful. Very peaceful. Like another world.'

'What is your work?' Yorgos asked.

'I'm an actor. But I'm thinking of giving it up.'

If he had been trying for her attention before, he had got it now. She stared at him, eyes wide, and he held her gaze.

Never, never in a million years could that remark be genuine! Acting had been his life even before she had first known him, and he had sacrificed everything, including her, to that ambition. He must have been able to read the blank disbelief in her eyes; his own seemed to hold a challenge. But the moment passed too quickly, and his attention was claimed by an excited Dimitri.

'Are you in films? Have you been to Hollywood? Are you famous?'

He laughed, his eyes still holding hers, and then turned to Dimitri beside him. 'Yes. Yes. No. . .obviously not, if you haven't heard of me!'

Dimitri looked puzzled by so many answers at once, and the others laughed. Even Nina was amused, though she avoided catching Hal's eye again. 'I didn't know you'd been to Hollywood,' she remarked, her tone carefully neutral.

'It's not surprising if you're no longer interested in actors and acting, as you said when we first talked.'

'You mean, I'd have read about you if I'd looked in the right magazines?'

'Not necessarily. The film wasn't exactly a box-office record breaker—just one of the many sci-fi adventure efforts. I did a couple of interviews at the time—one for a BBC film programme—and if you'd read or seen those you'd have heard about it.'

Anyone but Hal, and he would have intended to impress his audience with remarks like those. But his words were directed at her and she knew he was trying to find out if she had followed his career at any time, even though she had previously been at pains to suggest that she had not.

'What was it called?'

'*Black Neptune*. I was offered a part in it after the Stratford *Macbeth*. One wonders what peculiar train of associations encouraged the casting directors to pick on me.'

'*Macbeth*—witches—magic—black—Neptune?' she suggested. The remark was spontaneous, as was the smile that accompanied it, until Hal grinned back at her, his dark eyes sparkling with just that light of humour in them that she remembered from a shared past, when they used to play silly word association games late into the night.

It was just before eleven when the party broke up. There was no sign of the ferry, but it was invariably late and Yorgos and Katerina encouraged Nina to stay longer. She was certain that Hal would insist on waiting with her at the harbour, and wanted to avoid being alone with him for as long as possible, but she was unwilling to impose on the hospitality of Katerina—while she was there, the children wouldn't go to bed.

Also, although it was only a couple of minutes' walk down to the harbour, it would be a good idea to get there early. The ferry would anchor out in the little bay in deeper water, and travellers would have to transfer by fishing boat in which space was limited.

When the children finally allowed her to leave, she was kissed and hugged by Katerina and Elli, and Yorgos shook her hand warmly. 'We will see you again next year, Nina? We expect you!'

She was touched to think the family had accepted her in this way. 'Of course I'll be here—I've had a wonderful time!' Then she thought, Until yesterday. Until Hal turned up!

Dimitri, despite his mother, insisted on accompanying them down to the harbour, and Nina was glad of his presence. The longer he stayed with her, the less time she would have alone with Hal.

She had made one futile attempt to get rid of him. 'There's no need to come down with me, really. I'd rather wait on my own.'

'I'm staying down at the harbour, remember? And you'll get bored hanging round the taverna. The ferry won't be in for ages yet.'

She had been annoyed, and had let it show. 'I'm used to it—I have been here before, you know! Anyway, Dimitri is going to wait with me.'

'Only until half-past eleven—isn't that right, Dimitri?' And Hal had given her a thoughtful smile.

Packing had taken scarcely five minutes, and she had emerged from her room only to find Hal beside her, his hand instantly covering hers on the grips of the light holdall. The unexpected contact had made her flinch, and she had been aware of every inch of his tall, athletic frame as he had stood half behind her, his right hand over hers.

She had let go instantly and had pulled her hand away, unwilling to make a scene in front of the Greeks while Hal had taken his leave of them, writing his name on a hastily produced scrap of paper for Elli as her first genuine autograph.

They went down to the taverna and sat drinking small cups of rich Greek coffee, while Nina sat in silence, listening to Dimitri boasting of his escapades with friends, swimming and climbing round the island. She was amused by his blatant admiration of Hal, and impressed, despite herself, by the matter-of-fact way in which Hal dealt with it. Far from basking in the innocent flattery of the boy, it was he who constantly turned the subject away from the glamorous film world and encouraged Dimitri to talk about himself.

When he left, at Hal's insistence and not much after his mother's deadline, there was still no sign of the ferry. Nina hoped that her determined silence would drive Hal away, but he seemed quite relaxed, sitting back in his chair, a cigarette between the fingers of the hand that was resting idly on the table.

In the end she couldn't bear his silent study of her any longer. 'You never used to smoke.' He took a long pull at the cigarette, half closing his eyes as he did so, still watching her, and then blew out the smoke casually on a long breath before he spoke. 'That's what the stage does to you. A lot of waiting around, a lot of tension. I'm trying to give it up.'

'Looks like it,' she said sarcastically. 'Or did you mean the stage.'

'Both.' there was another pause, and then he said, 'You never used to be so nasty.'

'So you said yesterday.' She hesitated, and then added quickly, 'Look, Hal—there's no point in this. We're not going to meet again, so why pretend we've got anything to say to each other?'

She watched while he stubbed out the cigarette in a metal ashtray. Then he leaned back in his chair, and put his hands in the pockets of his jeans. 'Because we *have* got something to say to each other. Quite a lot, in fact——'

'Don't start raking up the past again!'

'I wasn't going to. I was going to talk about the future.'

'There isn't one—not for us.' Perhaps this time, instead of just defending, she should try an attack on different ground. Before he could comment, she asked, 'Are you really going to give up acting?'

He studied her a moment. 'Do you want to know the answer to that question, or are you talking for the sake of it?'

Her eyes sparked for a moment in annoyance then, her voice deliberately cool, she said, 'I asked because I was interested. But if you'd prefer to talk about the weather. . .?'

'No,' he said slowly. 'It's just that you've been very keen to avoid asking me anything up to now. . . You were surprised when I said earlier this evening that I was thinking of giving up, and you don't sound as though you believe it.'

'I don't. You were obsessed with the whole actor's world long before I knew you. You wanted big parts, lots of work, success in a big way. Why should you give it up now when you're getting all those things you've worked for?'

He was silent so long that she thought he wasn't going to answer her. When he finally did begin to speak, what he said lacked his characteristic fluency. There were many breaks and pauses as though, for once, he wasn't sure of his lines.

'I don't know if you'll understand what I'm going to say. Or whether I can even explain it. I thought that once you were almost as keen on it all as I was, but it seems that the glamour wore off for you long before it did for me. And there was always another part I wanted to play—another success I wanted to have.' He stopped, and lit a second cigarette. 'One success spurs you on to look for another. But. . .well, it's easy to lose touch with yourself—always faking emotions you don't feel, trying to get under the skin of a character that's entirely alien to you until you begin to think like him, and react like him, even off-stage. You find yourself speaking words that aren't really yours even in ordinary conversations.'

'Like now?'

'He gave her a direct look. 'No. Not like now.' He glanced down at the cigarette building its column of ash between his fingers, and gave a wry smile. 'I'm not aware of borrowing what I'm saying from any character I've played, but perhaps that's where the danger lies—it's become second nature to me. Who do you think I sound like?'

'No one. I just wondered.' She found herself watching the cigarette too. 'But you must have known this before—it's an occupational hazard. Why does it suddenly matter so much to you when it looks as though you could be a really big success? That's what you wanted.'

'Life in the fast lane, a hyped-up existence—rarely sleeping in the same bed for two nights running, for one reason or another. And in that world mostly *another*,' he added cynically. 'Do I really want to look back on a couple of divorces, a succession of women I can hardly remember, and half-relationships with my children who don't even know me?'

'It doesn't have to be like that.' Again, despite herself, her interest was held. She could still find herself becoming involved if she wasn't careful.

'No,' he agreed. 'Especially now when I have other options open to me. But will I be able to make the same decision at forty, or forty-five, when success has turned out the way I thought it would?'

'These options,' she said thoughtfully, 'are they just vague ideas, or do you really have choices to make?'

'For a long time now I've been a sort of "sleeping partner" in a business venture with a friend. He wanted to open up a small research development organisation and I put some capital into it. I'd just made a lot of money out of a film, and it seemed like a good idea at the time. I'd bought a house—though I've never had time to live in the place—and there was still a lot of money lying around spare. The thing's really taken off, and there's room for me to play a much more active role in the company.'

'But you're not interested in business!' she protested.

'How would you know that?' he said quietly. 'As you said yourself, five years is a long time.'

There was another silence. Hal finished the cigarette, and she watched him once again stub it out. She needed time to think; what he had just shown her of himself had been totally at odds with her image of him. This was a more thoughtful, serious man than the one she had known, facing some sort of personal crisis. Unwilling though she was to give any sign of it, there was still a ready sympathy in her that instinctively reached out towards him.

She waited for him to speak again, and a tension crept into the silence between them. He was sitting forward now, arms resting on the table, and hands loosely linked in front of him.

At last, looking at his hands, he spoke again. 'I want to change my life, Nina. I want the kind of stability I've never had, and life to have some sort of meaning beyond performance and success. I have some very good friends, but the life I lead isn't conducive to making new ones—not real friends, anyway.' He hesitated, and that deep, smooth voice was dangerously rough when he spoke again. 'There is no woman in my life, and something I've discovered since I saw you on this island is that there never really has been—since you.'

Nina felt as though her heart had suddenly dropped somewhere into the pit of her stomach. 'That's ridiculous, Hal!'

'Is it? I don't think so. You were everything I wanted. From the day I met you, I don't think I ever seriously considered anyone else. Since then I've been trying to find you in every woman I've been with. Why did you leave?'

She could hardly breathe. Her throat ached and her

mouth felt dry. She couldn't answer his question, but even though it sounded cruel she forced herself to say, 'I don't want you. I told you, it finished five years ago.'

His eyes seemed to be burning her. The gold of that Elizabethan earring glinted in the taverna lights. 'There's no man in your life.' It was a statement, not a question.

'How do you know?' she flung at him.

'Because you'd have told me if there had been—good ammunition to keep me at a distance. You've changed, Nina, but you're not as indifferent as you'd like to pretend.'

All the tension in her snapped suddenly—he was impossible! 'I don't know how I'm going to get this through to you!' she exclaimed, her anger defensive. 'I have my job, my life in Cambridge, my friends—and I'm perfectly contented with it all. It's a calm, peaceful life, which is something I've wanted for a long time. Whatever we had only happened because I was too young to know any better.' She knew the words were callous but it was better this way—it had to be final. 'I don't want it any longer. I don't even want to remember it.' She was looking at him now, her eyes blazing with an intensity that arrested him. There was something in his look that was almost startled.

'The best thing you can do,' she continued, 'if you care about me at all—as you say you do—is leave me alone!'

'We'll see.'

She stared at him a few seconds longer—open hostility in her eyes meeting quiet determination in his—and then, luckily, was saved from the need to reply by the stir amongst the other tourists at the taverna. The ferry, blazing with lights against the dark sea, had just slipped into view round the curve of the bay. People were pushing back their chairs and collecting their bags. Nina got up quickly.

'Sit down,' Hal said. 'There's no need to move yet.'

'I don't want to be last—the fishing boat's always crowded.' Any excuse to get away from him. She was dreading the moment when they would say goodbye, unless she could put some distance—and preferably three or four tourists—between them first.

Hal had dumped her bag beside his chair when they had sat down. She cursed herself for not having thought of an excuse to move it sooner. She had to bend towards him to retrieve it, and he reached out, his fingers circling her arm. 'It looks as though we're going to have to wait until we're both back in England before we can finish this conversation.'

He was getting to his feet. She tried to move away but he still had hold of her arm. She had to get the farewells over as quickly, and as formally, as possible.

'Goodbye, Hal. I hope everything works out for you—that your business succeeds, if that's what you want.' She didn't look him in the eyes, bending even as she spoke to pick up her bag. But, before she could touch it, he pulled her towards him and, caught off balance, she fell against him.

Then his arms were round her, and she felt herself being held close against the lean, muscular body. One hand was in her hair, and he pulled her head back until she was forced to meet his eyes. 'There is a future for us, Nina, and one day you're going to admit it. See you in England.'

She knew what he was going to do, but there was no way she could twist out of his grasp or turn her head away, and her protest was stifled almost before she could make a sound. His kiss was very brief—all but over before she had time to resist the contact. Then his lips brushed her cheek, and she felt his beard prick her skin as he buried his face in her hair.

'See you in England,' he repeated, and then let her go. The release was so unexpected that she staggered back against the table, staring at him wide-eyed, her breath coming in gasps. Even in those few seconds her body had registered their brief contact, but she had been preparing herself for a far more prolonged attack. Now, somewhere inside her, a perverse little voice was telling her of her secret disappointment that it hadn't lasted longer.

For an instant Hal looked as surprised as she, and then he smiled and picked up her bag. 'Come on. Let's load you on to the fishing boat.'

He didn't try to touch her again, and her 'Goodbye' was spoken as she turned from him to climb aboard the small transfer vessel. She didn't want to look at him again, and she didn't search for him as the boat pulled away from the little jetty, although she knew that he was still standing there.

Once on the ferry, she found a seat on which she could stretch out for the night in one of the saloons, and prepared herself for the voyage back to Piraeus.

She didn't even watch as the ferry headed out from the brightly lit little harbour to see the tall, bearded man standing on the jetty, hands in the pockets of his jeans, long after the other tourists had dispersed.

CHAPTER FOUR

'HANSEN and Averill Tutors—can I help you?' Nina pulled a face at Jenny across the desk, and then raised her eyes to heaven as a familiar voice of complaint launched into a monologue that left no opening for discussion. 'Mrs West again,' she mouthed at Jenny, and then struggled to keep the laughter out of her voice as her friend mimed to the irate quacking audible from the other end of the line.

Monday had started as it obviously meant to go on—with a succession of problem calls. It was still only half-past ten.

Nina put her hand over the mouthpiece. 'She's on about Tom Hunter again—she doesn't think he's teaching algebra properly now. Just get me Tom's file from the top shelf, could you? Sorry, Mrs West—what was that?'

She watched Jenny reach up to the top row on the neatly stacked metal shelving that lined the far office wall. It was time she re-sorted those tutors' files—it was getting increasingly difficult to find things. Some of the information was on the newly acquired computer, but not enough as yet to be useful, and she had found it hard to apply herself to the task with any enthusiasm since her return from Greece.

It was only after lengthy negotiation that she finally dropped the receiver with a look of profound relief. 'I don't know why that woman bothers to hire tutors from us if all she can do is complain about them!' she exclaimed in exasperation. 'It's her lazy little baggage of a daugher that's the problem, not people like Tom——' The phone rang again. '—I'm not answering it! If I don't get a cup of coffee soon I'll die—the thing's been ringing non-stop since about half-past eight.'

Jenny laughed, and paused to twist an unruly mop of brown curls up into the clips that had once restrained them. 'Shall I take a message? I'll say you're out for a while.'

'Thanks. Got time for a coffee?'

'I'd love one,' Jenny smiled, 'but mustn't hang about. Hello—Hansen and Averill Tutors. Can I help you?'

Nina left her partner's wife to lie her way in well-practised style through the next telephone conversation, and went to make the coffee. The large kitchen-dining-room had been built on to the back of the old terrace house her parents had given her, and she used the other two ground-floor rooms for business purposes: the back room was her office, and the front had been equipped with a couple of sofas and low tables as a reception room. She often had to interview clients, or prospective tutors, and occasionally Ed used it in the evenings as an additional study.

To make a distinction between the working and living parts of the house, she had decided to decorate the two work-rooms in as functional a style as possible. The back part of the house, and her own sitting-room and bedrooms upstairs, reflected more of her personality.

The kitchen, with its bright yellows and light-coloured cork floor, always cheered her when she went into it, and the clean Scandinavian lines of the furniture her father had given her lent the dining section a certain elegance. Now, however, the neat, stylish impression of the room was somewhat marred by the litter of jigsaw puzzle pieces and toys that strewed the floor.

A tousle-headed six-year-old looked up from under the table. His bright hazel eyes were Jenny's. 'I've lost a bit,' he announced.

Nina grinned at him, picking her way across the minefield on the floor to plug in the kettle. 'I'm not surprised, in that chaos! Why not give up looking for a while and do some more of the puzzle, and then you might find it as you go along?'

'I think it's gone,' he said gloomily. 'Is there anything on television? Where's Mum going?' There was no suppressed anxiety in his query about his mother and, as far as Tim was concerned, Nina's house was just an extension of home.

It gave her a secret sense of joy that he was happy to be left with her for hours on end if need be. Sometimes it was almost as though he were her own son.

She bent down to extract a carton of milk from the fridge. 'She's got to go to Ely for an audit.'

'What's that?'

'Counting up other people's money to make sure they've got their sums right. But we're having coffee first.'

There was a companionable silence while Nina waited for the kettle to boil and Tim reapplied himself to his search for the jigsaw piece. From where she was standing, one elbow propped on the work surface, she could see the missing section on its face underneath the table, and, after her carefully phrased suggestion, he pounced on it and held it up, beaming proudly. 'Found it!'

She watched him fit it in, and then he scrambled to

his feet to catch her round the legs, above the knees, looking up at her from under a heavy fringe of brown silky hair with what Jenny called 'his wheedling look'—Nina always found it irresistible. She was ready to agree instantly to whatever he asked, and in her position as friend of the family could afford to indulge him. Perhaps it was a good thing she wasn't his mother, she reflected now. She would have spoiled him. Tim, in many ways, was one of the most important elements in her life. When the child was around, she wasn't aware any longer of that void in her existence that nothing so far had been able to fill.

'Can we go to the park later?'

She ran a hand through his hair, smiling at his eagerness. 'Sure—but only for half an hour, I'm afraid. I have to be back here to answer the phone and see a new tutor this afternoon.'

She sighed, glancing out of the window as she turned to take a couple of mugs from the draining board. It would have been fun to spend the whole afternoon in the park with Tim, but Ed was in London and there was no one to look after the office.

Outside the kitchen window, her small walled garden had a definite October look. The Michaelmas daisies were festooned with cobwebs and a mist still hung over everything. The muted autumnal colours of shrubs and trees were a long way from the brilliant turquoise and sunlit whitewash of her Mediterranean summer.

The island, and everything that had happened on it, seemed like a dream now. But although she had tried to tell herself that the disturbance to her life she had feared from the reappearance of Hal had in reality been nothing more than a small ripple, their meeting still hung over her somehow. She was left with a new awareness of everything he had forced her to reconsider, and the threat of his reappearance in her life—something that could happen at any time, despite her unwillingness to re-establish any sort of relationship between them. And she had no doubt that he would find her if he meant to.

August and September had been unusually busy. First there were the extra foreign students looking for English lessons—she had rather left Ed in the thick of it this year by taking her Greek holiday a little later than usual. Then by September there were the unsuccessful exam candidates trying to arrange extra coaching before retakes, and now there was the new batch of foreigners, and assorted individuals wanting tutoring in a foreign language.

To add to the confusion, Ed sometimes took on extra work in the spring and summer for another organisation, helping to arrange two- to six-week language courses. He had much larger financial commitments than Nina herself, and, although the agency was doing quite well, often worried about money.

The kettle switched itself off as Jenny entered the kitchen. 'I've left the details of that last call on your desk,' she reported. 'Someone wanting an Italian tutor.'

Nina grinned. 'At least *something* seems to be going right! I'm just about to interview a woman this afternoon to do that very thing. Let's hope she's suitable. Sugar? Or is this another diet day?'

Jenny groaned. 'I weighed myself again last night, so the answer has to be no.'

'I wish you'd believe that there's nothing wrong with your figure!'

Jenny stared morosely into the black, unsweetened liquid in her mug. 'That's what I tell myself, until I look at you. And then I think of Ed working all day with a virtual fashion model, and I wonder if he's going to divorce me for being aesthetically incompatible. He likes thin women.'

An unexpected echo of a conversation she'd had with Hal only a couple of months ago was in Nina's mind. He'd remembered how hungry she used to get at night—'sticky cakes at midnight' was the phrase he'd used.

'I've always been skinny,' she said dismissively. 'There's no virtue in it. And Jenny, you're *not* fat. As for Ed divorcing you for anything—there's not even the remotest possibility! I've never known two happier people.'

'We're very lucky,' Jenny said thoughtfully. 'But then, I happen to think that marriage is a good institution. You should try it some time. . .you spend far too much time on your own.' Then she gave one of her attractive, friendly grins. 'As for my weight, my excuse is Timmy. Having a child is really disastrous—you never get back to a respectable shape again.'

Jenny couldn't know it, but marriage and children weren't subjects Nina allowed herself to think about very often—they were too inextricably tied up with Hal. She supposed she would marry, one day, but it wouldn't be until the past had receded to very much more dim and distant horizons than at present.

At first she said nothing, unwilling to open up a discussion on the matter. Then she started a new subject. 'I don't suppose you've got time to talk about that tax claim we made? We can't afford to pay any more tax than is absolutely necessary at the moment. Honestly, getting money out of the Inland Revenue is like getting water out of the Sahara—it's there all right, but you've got to know your way round the wells!'

Jenny laughed. 'That's just about it! But I won't go into the nitty gritty just now, if you don't mind. Don't lose any sleep over it—I'm sure I can work something out.'

'We have every confidence in you, my business partner and I!' Nina joked. 'But just bear in mind that we can't afford to lose very much at present, especially with that new tutoring agency opening up. We might have to spend more on advertising ourselves.'

Jenny put her empty mug down very firmly on the work surface. 'That coffee was just what I needed, but now I've got to love you and leave you. You wouldn't think that in theory I'd got the day off to look after Tim's cold, would you? Answering your business calls, rushing out to Ely at a moment's notice. . .thanks for looking after Tim again. See you later.' She bent down to drop a quick kiss on her son's head. 'Bye, sweetheart. Be good.' He didn't even glance up from his game.

The rest of the morning was passed between answering the phone and re-sorting the files, until Tim begged to play his new game on the computer.

As computers went, it was a fairly standard model. She and Ed had invested in it, in an attempt to cut down on time spent on paperwork, but they were far from using it to its full potential. Because it was still a novelty, she suspected that Ed had bought the new game as much for himself as for his son.

Their snack lunch was eaten during brief respite from the space war hostilities that Nina found every bit as engrossing as her six-year-old companion. She couldn't do anything about going out until the prospective Italian tutor turned up for interview, so she decided to enjoy herself.

It was already ten minutes beyond the interview time when there was a ring at the bell. She closed the office door on the computerised bleeps and whizzes and went to the front door, her 'business smile', as Ed called it, arranged on her face. Then the smile froze.

'Hello, Nina.'

'Hal. . .!' The word was barely a whisper. Just as before, the shock was physical. There had been that vague threat of his seeing her again, yes, but she'd never expected. . .!

She stared at him in sheer disbelief, but his presence, as always, affected her like wine in her blood.

Apart from the tan, which had faded, he looked very much as he had on the island—the earring and the beard were still the same. He was wearing a fashionably styled leather jacket and a pair of dark jeans, and his height seemed to fill the doorway.

There was silence between them for a moment, and then he said, 'Aren't you going to ask me in?'

'I. . .it's. . .' Every excuse seemed to have left her head. All she was aware of was that despite everything she was actually pleased to see him.

Hal gave a half-smile, his dark eyes watching her. 'For someone running a tutorial agency, you're remarkably elusive. I tried ringing up about an intensive course in businessmen's Japanese starting yesterday, but I've been forced to go to your rivals instead.'

Somehow she had retreated from that all too dominating presence, and somehow he was already in the hall.

'How. . .how did you find me?' she faltered, wondering if this wasn't a dream.

'The phone book, of course. There's only one tutorial agency with the name "Hansen" in it.'

At that moment there was a plaintive accusation

from the office. 'Hey—you said you were coming back!' And then Tim appeared, shoeless, the waist of his trousers as usual somewhere round his hips, and glared up at her from under the mop of dark hair. She was aware of Hal looking at him, and then watching her. 'You *said* you'd come back if it wasn't the new tutor!' Then he turned to Hal. 'You're not the Italian person, are you?'

Hal rattled off a mouthful of something incomprehensible, and Nina, thrown for a second by the unexpectedness of it, asked in surprise, 'You don't speak Italian, do you?'

He laughed, but it didn't quite ring true—she knew him too well to be taken in by it, and there was a curious look in his eyes that quite definitely wasn't amusement. 'No,' he replied qucikly, 'nor do you! That was off a menu.'

'Are you the Italian tutor?' Tim was persistent.

'No. I'm a friend of. . .Nina's.' It was that slight hesitation before he said her name that gave him away. 'Who are you?'

'Tim,' the child replied uncompromisingly, and meeting Hal's eyes she could read an almost agonised impatience in them, and knew why it was there. 'Come and play with me?'

'Sure—if you want me to. . .'

She took pity on him. 'He's Ed and Jenny's son,' she said quietly. 'Ed's my partner.'

'Yes. You told me about Ed—I remember.' Hal's expression had changed—he almost looked relieved.

The irony of his assumption that the child was hers and his subsequent reaction hurt her, but she didn't have time to dwell on it. At that moment, she became aware that they were being observed by a woman on the doorstep who obviously didn't know quite how to announce her presence. It was Timmy who had noticed her first.

In the end, Hal found himself involved in the on-going space war while Nina did her best to conduct a convincing interview. With almost her whole mind on Hal in the next room, she knew that she wasn't putting on a very creditable performance as a competent employer, and by the end would have found herself engaging the woman even if she had spoken nothing by Mongolian.

What on earth was she going to do about Hal? She hadn't considered very seriously how she'd cope if he did turn up again, preferring to forget about the whole thing when she could. But the few intervening months hadn't changed her mind about the impossibility of becoming further involved with him.

She would just have to treat him as a casual friend—that was the best way of avoiding any intense situations, and would be the most difficult kind of defence to penetrate. She'd also have to hope that his stay in Cambridge wouldn't be a long one.

Once the newly appointed tutor had left, she went back to the office, determined that the easiest way of coping with Hal for the present would be to go for the walk she and Tim had intended.

He was lounging in a chair beside Tim. They appeared absorbed in the space battle before them, but Hal looked up as she came into the room. She avoided his eyes.

'OK, Tim, get your coat—she's gone now and we can go to the park.'

'Can Hal come too?'

'Of course, if he really thinks he'd like playing on the swings.' She didn't mean to sound sarcastic and was relieved when Hal only grinned at her. Trying not to be too aware of him, she concentrated on the child. 'Come here a minute.' She lifted Tim up bodily by the waistband, pulling up the descending trousers by force. Normally it made him giggle, but now he frowned, resenting such intimacies in front of his new, grown-up friend. 'Where are your shoes?'

'I dunno,' he said unhelpfully. 'I had them this morning.' She was conscious of Hal's amused gaze as she hunted under the furniture in the office, and then in the front room. He followed her.

'Oh, hell,' she said. 'Are you sure you haven't left them upstairs, Tim? Try the sitting-room.'

The child looked rebellious for an instant, and then caught her eye. 'No shoes, no walk,' she said firmly.

Hal made no effort to hide the fact that he was well entertained. 'I've thought about you a lot since the summer,' he said, 'but I never imagined you in quite such a domestic role! It suits you.'

It was comments like that that she would have to prepare herself for. She turned away to hide anything her face might betray. In Tim's temporary absence, she was beginning to feel acutely awkward in his company, and went into the kitchen to continue the search for the missing shoes—merely to have something to occupy her. Hal followed.

He perched on one of the kitchen stools, looking aggravatingly cool, and she wished that she could do something to break the tension that was mounting in herself. It had a lot to do with all those dangerous reefs that had lain just below the surface of their conversation that summer, but on some deeper level, well below conscious thought, her body was reacting to his proximity. She felt nervous and ill at ease, and her hand shook as she reached to tidy away the cups from beside the sink just to give herself something to do.

'So, how's the business?'

'Fine, thanks.'

There was another silence. She nearly dropped a saucer, and, to cover the awkwardness, asked, 'How's the acting? You look very pleased with yourself.' She regretted that remark.

'That's because I'm seeing you.' He was watching her to see how she took it. She didn't let her face show anything.

'But on the subject of acting,' he continued, 'it's going very well at the moment. The company's here for two weeks'—two weeks!—'with three plays. We finished the last run a bit early, which is why I'm here with lots of time to see you until Thursday—that's our first night. Are you coming?'

'I haven't time.' It was a lie, and he must know it, but it was hard to find any sensible reply with him sitting there.

'It's a play by Webster—one of the ones I got the earring for. You used to like Webster.'

They weren't going to get on at all, even for half an hour in the park, if he was going to remind her all the time of the things she wanted to forget!

'I used to like a lot of things,' she replied, deliberately cold, warning him off. 'I don't any more.'

He shrugged, and smiled, evidently undeterred by her reception of him. 'That's a pity.'

That deep, rich voice, as always, ran through her. She turned away abruptly. 'I'm going to get my jacket. I don't recommend the park.'

'Why not? Because you've decided I'm one of the things you don't like any more?'

She was half-way out of the kitchen door. 'You'll be bored,' she said crushingly. 'There's nothing very thrilling about slides and swings.' She expected him to laugh it off, but there was only silence as she bolted upstairs to fetch her coat.

Tim appeared on the landing with his shoes on the wrong feet. Something she didn't care to analyse prompted her to hug him rather than argue with him. He was surprised. 'I can't breathe!' he protested. 'Let go. Can I take my catapult?'

He cross-questioned her on the subject of Hal while she swapped the shoes round, and went downstairs with the firm intention of interviewing a real movie actor about space adventures—she wondered whether Hal would be flattered or insulted.

She glanced at herself in the mirror as she slipped on the light, navy wool jacket that was more or less a match for the well-cut trousers she had put on that morning. She looked very pale now—her Mediterranean tan had long faded, and there was a hint of strain about her eyes. Probably worry about Ed's finances, she told herself. She certainly hadn't wasted time brooding on her own situation up to now—there'd been too much to do.

She repinned the swathe of long, silvery-fair hair on top of her head, and wondered whether to add a touch of make-up to give colour to her face.

'But who am I trying to impress anyway?' she demanded of the image that stared back at her. 'Certainly not Hal!' It wasn't strictly true, and she knew it: there were too many contradictions in the way she was feeling about her former lover. But she told herself that she wasn't going to let him think she'd gone to pieces since their meeting in the summer. Or that her life wasn't in its own way just as successful as his.

Her eyes, pale aquamarine flecked with darker colour round the pupils, stared back at her—they seemed unnaturally large, framed by their black lashes.

She had lost weight; even her face showed it. She couldn't really afford to lose any more. . . Carefully, she was avoiding thinking too much about Hal, waiting for her downstairs.

She would just have to forget that they'd ever had a past, and meet each situation as it came. That wouldn't be difficult for a couple of hours, surely! Especially when she didn't really know how she felt—half resentful that he had sought her out, and half afraid of what might result. No, that didn't fully define it either—somewhere in the confusion of it all she was almost pleased.

'Nina! Aren't you ready yet?' Tim, impatient, interrupted her thoughts. She glanced round the sitting-room for his coat, and then remembered that it was in the office.

He was fully dressed and hopping from foot to foot at the bottom of the stairs. 'Hal did my coat for me. Can't we go yet?'

Automatically, she fished first one glove and then the other out of his pockets, and put them on to his hands, her mind unexpectedly full of a new image of Hal—he had had no time for children in the past. She was conscious of him watching her.

During the walk to the park, an animated conversation was carried on almost exclusively between Tim and Hal—she couldn't have got a word in edgeways if she'd tried, and was grateful for it. The presence of the child eased the awkwardness of Hal's sudden reappearance in her life. Tim seemed to have taken to the tall, bearded stranger in a big way; he was prepared to hold his hand trustingly when crossing roads, and showed no inclination to run ahead or interview stray dogs as he did with her.

Despite herself, she was impressed by Hal's easy,

relaxed attitude to the little boy, and the park, from the latter's point of view at least, was an unqualified success. It was deserted but for them, and she sat on a roundabout while Tim ran in mysterious circles of his own. Hal, covering the ground in long, easy strides, came to stand beside her.

'Want a ride? I'll push you if you'll push me.' Watching the child just then, it didn't occur to her to be wary of him.

'You're just as much of a baby as Tim!' she exclaimed. 'You've come here to have a good play—and I don't mean the acting kind!' She was genuinely amused, and her eyes, full of quiet laughter, met his. There was a moment's silence between them.

'I remember a time when you liked messing about in children's playgrounds!' he countered, with a smile. But she couldn't interpret the look in his eyes. 'Who was it who was showing off to me turning somersaults on a slide and then fell off at the bottom?' He was teasing her, remembering the way they had both played—two students pretending to be children. Then she had been totally uninhibited, laughing, daring him to jump off a swing higher and further than she could or walk along the edge of a high boundary wall. They had entered into the spirit of it equally, knowing all along that they were playing a different, more adult game.

She laughed at him now, for one unguarded moment the old Nina. 'Show-off yourself! Who was pretending to be Tarzan on a children's climbing frame and pulled a muscle in his shoulder?'

In reply, he gave the roundabout a sudden shove and she found herself unexpectedly facing the trees instead of him, and then Tim came running up to join them and put an effective end to any further reminiscence.

They couldn't pretend that they'd never had a past—perhaps Hal was right in that. But as long as it was only the good bits they talked about and she could keep everything else safely hidden, and as long as he didn't want to make out that there was a future for them, they might even enjoy each other's company as a sort of brief interlude before their very separate existences claimed them again. Then she realised she was already making concessions to him.

But as she watched the man and the child kicking up dead leaves, and then Tim swinging from Hal's arm, both of them enjoying themselves, her mood changed. She couldn't wholly ignore the bittersweet feeling deep down inside her that Hal, and the boy she regarded almost as her own son, should so clearly find delight in each other's company. Her heart ached for what might have been.

'What are you doing tomorrow night?' Hal asked, in the middle of a three-way conversation about adventures as they walked home.

Without thinking, she replied, 'Nothing——' and then regretted it. He was too good at catching her out.

'We're having dinner—I'll call round for you at seven.'

'But Hal——'

'No "buts",' he said quietly. 'I'll call round for you anyway, so you might as well give in gracefully.' He looked across at her, over the child between them. She met his eye, and knew that there was no point arguing. There never had been, when he was determined about something.

* * *

Tim was contentedly asleep in the spare room by the time Ed appeared to collect him after eight o'clock that evening. Nina wasn't worried. Jenny had phoned on the way back from Ely to say that the car had broken down, and she hadn't expected Ed back until much later.

'Where is everybody?' he demanded, striding into the sitting-room where Nina was lying on the sofa with her feet up, watching television. He had a key to the house, and she had heard him on the stairs. 'No one at home, and everyone out having fun. I guessed they'd both be round here.'

Ed was only a little taller than Nina, wiry and packed with simmering energy. His lean face invariably wore an expression of good humour.

Nina smiled at him, and stretched her arms behind her head. 'Your son's asleep in the spare room and Jenny rang about an hour ago, waiting for a garage man—somewhere between here and Ely with a burst hose.'

Ed was taking off his raincoat. 'You mean she could actually identify it?' he asked incredulously. 'Poor old Jen. And what about the Offspring? Any trouble?'

Nina got up to turn off the television. 'Good as gold. Like a drink?' She held up a bottle of Scotch.

He gave an exaggerated sigh of satisfaction. 'Mind-reader. Anything so long as it's alcoholic. That'll do beautifully. I came here on my bike. Can I borrow your car to take him home?'

'Of course,' she replied warmly. 'Bring your bike through the house and leave it in the back garden for the night. You don't want it pinched from the street.' She watched him slump back in his chair, legs stretched out before him, in an attitude of casual comfort. Like Tim, he treated the house very much as a second home. If she'd had a brother, she liked to imagine that he'd be an Ed.

'Something tells me we ought to get rid of that damn car before the winter sets in,' he went on glumly. 'But there's this tiny problem called money.'

'You know you can always use my car. I hardly ever need it.'

'Thanks, Nina. I know you mean that, but we couldn't take advantage of it. We'll have to get a new one some time.'

'Then things are seriously tight?' It wasn't the first discussion they'd had on the topic.

He took a long pull at the whisky. 'If Jen couldn't pay the mortgage, we'd be out on the street. Well, no, it's not quite that bad. We needn't have taken on such a big house. Anyway, I made a few enquiries at that meeting today, and one of the international language schools could be looking for a course director soon. The salary's tempting, and the base is London or Cambridge.'

It was something that she had been dreading. Ed was so much more than just a partner—he and Jenny were part of her whole pattern of existence.

'It's not just a question of the car, though—there's Tim's future schooling, repairs to the roof of the house. . .and, you know, lots of little things running down, and no spare cash. Don't look so quiet and withdrawn all of a sudden—it may never happen. It's only a thought so far.'

'If you wanted to go, Ed, I wouldn't try to make trouble over the partnership.'

'I know you wouldn't, honey. And I wouldn't even be thinking of it if I suspected you were going to come badly out of it. But you're quite capable of running the thing on your own, especially if you took on a couple of people to help you. We'll ask Jenny about the finances of it some time.'

But she knew she would have not the slightest interest in carrying on with the agency if Ed left. Despite her efficiency and good business sense, it was Ed's drive and ambition that kept her going. She wanted the agency to succeed for him and Jenny, but, even before that meeting with Hal in the summer had brought her life into sharper focus, she had known that for herself she didn't really care.

'And now, what's today's news? You and Tim truanting in Cambridge?'

She gave a brief account of their expedition with Hal, merely alluding to him as 'someone I used to know ages ago', and then the discussion drifted back on to the subject of business until Ed got up to leave.

'I'd better think about getting the son and heir home—I hope you don't mind, but I'll have to bring him with me again tomorrow; Jenny thought we shouldn't send him back to school for another day.'

Nina smiled a little wistfully. 'Of course I don't mind. I really love having him here, you know that. I just wish you'd leave him sometimes.'

'I often think the Averill family takes up far too much of your living space and your life—you never get any time off from us!'

You three *are* my life! Nina thought, but she didn't say it.

He reached for his coat, hanging across the banisters, and took the keys of her car from her.

While he was outside starting it up she went upstairs to find Tim, still sleeping, his striped T-shirt rucked up round his chest and one arm flung out over the pillow. She of all people had no right to wish she could keep him there, but for one instant found herself longing for the impossible.

She heard Ed come up the stairs, two at a time in his usual manner.

'Asleep?' he queried.

She nodded. 'He's still got his clothes on, I'm afraid. He refused to take them off.'

Ed grinned. 'There's modesty for you. It's his latest phase. We'll get them off him in the morning. Did he bring any stuff?'

Tim scarcely murmured as Ed wrapped him in the duvet, and picked up the cocoon to carry him downstairs.

'Should anyone called Jenny Averill drop in, just remind her that she's married to me, would you, and tell her that she lives somewhere in the direction of the Madingley Road? I haven't seen her around much lately.' He was grinning as he spoke. 'Thanks again for looking after this—see you tomorrow.'

Once he and Tim had gone, the house felt abandoned. The thought haunted her that Ed might be looking for a job that would take him and Jenny and their child out of the everyday companionship she had come to value so much. The job without them would be mere drudgery. And beyond the job?

She rarely allowed herself to feel depressed, but now, suddenly, she found herself wondering what her life was really all about—what was the point in working for a success you didn't care about?

'Don't be such a weed!' she told herself firmly. She'd be crying in a minute, and that was something she rarely did. She couldn't even remember the last—oh, yes, she could. . . A sunlit beach, when Hal had forced her to relive things she'd deliberately buried deep—so deep that uncovering them again had cost her a pain that was almost physical.

Hal. And now he was there again. She had tried to blank him from her mind after Greece—what had been the point in remembering? But now he seemed determined to find his way back into her life. She would avoid him if she could, even though she had to admit she'd enjoyed his unexpected reappearance today. But then they'd had the child to defuse any unwelcome tensions that would have been there without him. Thinking of the past, it was ironical how it was Tim who had brought them together again for a few hours.

When the telephone rang she jumped, instantly thinking that it might be Hal. Tension, as she picked up the phone, seemed almost to crackle on the line.

'Nina—it's me, Jen. I just wanted you to know I got back all right. Thanks a million for looking after Tim—I hope you don't mind him again tomorrow. I'm really sorry, but they just won't let me take any more time off.'

'Of course I don't mind—you know that.'

'You're a darling.' Jenny's voice sounded warm, full of affection and contentment. She heard Ed's low murmur in the background, then Jenny said, 'Ed says you've qualified for your hundredth harp and crown and he'll give you a bottle of Scotch because he thinks he's drunk most of yours.'

'I'm glad you got back OK. Thanks for ringing, Jenny.'

'It's the least I could do—night.'

She stood for a while, just staring at the telephone, images of Ed and Jenny coming to her mind. She could imagine them in the untidy, cosy sitting-room of the big Victorian house they'd bought. The phone was by the sofa, and they must have been sitting together. Ed might even have lit a fire as he liked doing in the evenings. They were together, and their child was asleep upstairs. All the comfortable domesticity she'd tried to persuade herself she'd never wanted.

Then she went to bed, but for a long time she lay awake, thinking of Ed and Jenny. Of their little son, barely six years old. And of Hal.

CHAPTER FIVE

SHE wasn't going to let him take over the initiative this time. She'd had over twenty-four hours to regret her agreement to go out with him, and that was long enough to work out a way to deal with the situation.

'Hal,' she said as she opened the door to him. 'Let's pretend we're strangers—we only just met yesterday and you asked me out to dinner because you fancied me or something.'

'I do fancy you——'

'We've got no past,' she cut across him firmly. 'And we'll talk about the things that ordinary strangers would talk about. All right? Otherwise I'm staying right here, and you can spend the rest of the evening outside on the doormat for all I care!'

One dark eyebrow lifted in something that looked like amused surprise. 'OK. If that's the way you want to play it. But there's no call to be so aggressive. There's one thing I need to know, though. . .'

'What's that?' she asked, a little warily.

'Am I allowed to fancy you or not?' He was looking her up and down, dark eyes assessing, with just a hint of a smile in them.

'Definitely not, if it means you're going to do or say anything I don't like—and I warn you, I won't be waiting around for apologies!'

He gave an exaggerated groan, but she suspected that he was already entering into the spirit of it. 'This promises to be a disastrous evening—how will I know when I'm on dangerous ground?'

'You won't,' she said sweetly. 'Just make sure you don't stray from your role of polite and well-behaved stranger. Shall we go?'

She remembered then how she had been angry with him on the island for staging things. Now acting a part was precisely what she was recommending for both of them. But this time she was the one who intended to write the script, not he, and she wasn't going to allow him to take the lead away from her.

She had wasted a lot of time wondering why she was letting him take her out in the first place. The only explanation seemed to have something to do with feelings that she didn't want to admit. In the end, she evaded the issue by telling herself that he would only pester her until she gave in, and that would just make the whole situation increasingly unpleasant. If they could meet casually on her terms this time then they need disturb none of those deeper levels she had tried, without success, to avoid in the summer.

So she took over the conversation from the moment she got into his car—a long, low power-machine parked just outside—telling him about Cambridge and the agency before he'd had a chance to open his mouth. All the way to the restaurant she dwelt on the more humorous aspects of the early difficulties there had been in setting up the business, when she had managed all the office affairs and Ed had been the sole tutor, and the topic continued over dinner.

'It sounds as though it was a lot of fun,' he commented.

'It was—when we weren't worried about where the next pupil was coming from. And it got quite tricky when one of us was ill. I even found myself teaching an Italian business man once when Ed had flu in the early days.'

He looked surprised. 'Do you have any qualifications?'

She laughed. 'Of course not! Ed just told me to look as though I knew what I was doing, and claim I was giving "conversation classes".'

'So you haven't lost your talent for acting!' Then he caught her warning glance. 'Sorry——' he said quickly. 'Delete that remark—it just slipped out! So what happened?' It was safest to ignore that allusion to their past. She went on, 'It wasn't much of a success as far as language lessons went, but the man's English seemed quite good enough to me on the only topics that interested him—like "How old are you? Will you come out with me? Have you got a boyfriend?"!'

'And had you?' he asked carefully.

She met his eyes across the table, her own deliberately blank. 'Of course not.' Her voice was suddenly without animation. 'I was far too busy working to have time to go out with anyone.'

'Then in my role of "stranger",' he said, 'I'm going to comment that you're far too attractive to spend your time cooped up in an office all day. You must have gone out with somebody some time?'

'Then in *my* role of "stranger" I'm going to tell you that I never give away all my secrets on first acquaintance.'

'Does this mean that you might come out with me again?'

'Only if you behave yourself!' she countered neatly. She was well in control of the situation this time—they could go on like this indefinitely; it was quite safe. She just withdrew behind the part she was playing whenever he stepped out of line. There seemed no reason now why she should go out of her way to avoid him in the future. She was even quite enjoying herself in his company.

They left the restaurant late, and Hal drove her back to the house. She had no intention of asking him in, and he made no suggestion of it, merely telling her that he'd try to see her again when the rest of the company turned up.

'Thursday's our first night, and they're due tomorrow. They've been rehearsing a new play for the last couple of days. I'm not in it so I decided to come on ahead and enjoy myself.'

'And are you?'

'Am I what—enjoying myself? When I get to take out lovely "strangers" like you, I'm not complaining. And, speaking as a stranger at the end of our first proper date, am I allowed to kiss you?' He had turned half towards her, one arm resting on the wheel, and she could see his eyes glitter in the subdued street light that filtered into the car.

She opened the door rather quickly. 'No,' she said firmly. 'Goodnight, Hal!'

He gave a rueful grin. 'It was worth asking, anyway!'

She watched the tail-lights of the Porsche until it turned the corner, and then put her key in the lock of the front door. She couldn't help suspecting that what she was doing as far as Hal was concerned would end up best described as 'playing with fire'. . . But it made a change from spending her evenings with the computer! she told herself. And anyway, she wasn't going to let anything happen.

She didn't see him at all the next day, even though she half expected it, but she had found an envelope on the mat that morning containing a ticket for a play called *The White Devil*. He had told her it was the first of three they were performing at the Arts Theatre. There was no note with the ticket, but no doubt as to who had sent it.

She wasn't sure whether to feel irritated or pleased that Hal didn't try to see her again immediately. She ought to be telling herself that the longer he stayed away from her, the better, but she had enjoyed having dinner with him, despite everything. He had obviously been making an effort to please her, and she had never been indifferent to his charm.

'We can't make any real money at this until we take over some big residential place, and run our own holiday language packages,' Ed complained later that morning.

They were struggling with the preliminary arrangements for the Easter language course, and he was still doubtful about his financial situation.

Now he tapped his pencil absent-mindedly on the desk top. 'I still look through the ads from time to time for nice little language school directorships—even assistant directorships. . . Being your own boss in this set-up has its drawbacks.'

Increasingly, Nina was dreading a time when he might decide to pull out of the partnership, but Ed and Jenny were her friends—she would never stand in the way of their interests.

'Seen anything hopeful lately?' she asked encouragingly, successfully hiding her own sinking feeling that he just might have done.

'Only Eastbourne,' he said glumly. 'That conjures up visions of lots of elderly ladies with unattractive dogs on the promenade off-season. Jenny'd never survive it.'

If either of them could survive it, it would be Jenny, she thought privately. It was Ed who would find it intolerable. She switched back again. 'But the prospects for our new French student venture with Monsieur Whatsisname were good, weren't they?'

'Leclair. Yes. We ought to look on the bright side.'

'And we could ring up Jenny and ask her to find us a few more tax-deductibles.'

He brightened up. 'Nothing like having your very own accountant on hand—except that she isn't this week. Oh. . .'

She guessed that that was a preliminary to a favour he had forgotten to ask her, and suspected that it would have something to do with picking up Tim from school. It had.

'Only it might be a bit later than usual tomorrow,' he added apologetically. 'There's something on there. He wasn't very clear about it.'

Tomorrow's date was on the ticket Hal had sent her for *The White Devil*. Still, Tim's school wouldn't make any difference even if it kept her late—she had no intention of going near the theatre.

She worked on her own in the office all the next day, catching up on correspondence and straightening out more of the filing. Then she got ready to fetch Tim. She needed a walk, but it would be quicker to take the car, and less tiring for the child. It was unexpectedly sunny and bright outside, and she wouldn't need a coat. She slipped on a loose, brightly coloured jersey over her silk blouse. It looked a bit too casual for her slim dark skirt and high heels, but there wasn't time to change properly. At least it would catch Tim's eye if he forgot who was collecting him.

There were more vehicles than she had expected in the school car park, but, although she looked for the clusters of mothers waiting by the main doors to the cloakrooms, with the usual assortment of bicycles, push-chairs and younger children, there was no one. Then she remembered that Ed had said there was something on. She made her way into the building and down a long corridor that led to the offices and assembly hall.

One of the secretaries was standing by the doors to the hall when she reached it, having an unofficial look at whatever was happening inside. She turned to geet Nina.

'It looks quite a success, doesn't it?' she said, nodding towards the hall. There were shouts of children, and then a lot of laughter. 'Why not go in and watch while you're waiting? Who have you come to collect?'

'Timothy Averill. What is it?' There were too many adults standing with their backs to her for her to be able to glimpse what was happening.

'Oh, we've got that wonderful new company of actors in from the Arts Theatre for a Drama Afternoon. They get bookings from lots of schools in the towns they visit. They're doing some mime for the children. Go and have a look. I'd stay and watch but I'll be missed in the office. Do go in.' The secretary was already opening the door for her. Unthinkingly, Nina obeyed, although seeing Hal act was one of the things she wanted to avoid—it would bring her too close to the past. But there was something about people who worked in schools, a sort of bright bossiness, that it was almost impossible to resist.

There was a mime going on between three masked characters that was holding the children enthralled. The actors had dispensed with the stage, and were in the middle of the floor, surrounded by the eager audience, some sitting on the floor itself, others perched on chairs.

The mime involved a comic argument between one of the characters, a pugnacious and clumsy individual, and the other two who were quicker and more agile, darting in to offer gestured insults and bops on the head with a balloon.

She didn't have to see the face of one of the more agile actors to know who it was—the tall, lithe body with its athletic grace was unmistakable. Instinctively she shrank back behind the women in front of her. Hal in his professional context was something she couldn't yet come to terms with—but she felt compelled to stay and watch despite herself.

More balloons appeared and found their way among the children, and the whole mime ended in a joyous free-for-all between audience and actors.

After that the performers took off their masks, and Hal, with enviable professional skill, succeeded in quieting a mob of over-excited primary school children within seconds. He didn't even have to raise his voice. Its beautiful, rich tones were like a spell that wove itself around and through them all before she or they were even aware of it. He was telling a story, and she was drawn to listen.

At first she stared at the floor, trying to cope with some of the feelings the sound of his deep, mellow voice immediately woke in her, but after a while she raised her eyes to watch him, totally relaxed as he was with one foot on a chair and hands linked round his knee. The gestures he made were fluid and economical, evoking images of the story almost like a dancer.

He had the trick of appearing to talk to each member of the audience individually, and gradually involved some of them in the process of story-telling. With his strong-featured, dark-bearded face, and the turquoise in his ear, he was exactly like some fascinating character out of a child's adventure himself, despite the conventional jeans and dark sweatshirt.

Twice his eyes met hers, but she wondered if he was

truly aware of her. When it ended there was a riot of applause, and then one of his companions, introduced as Nick, began another mime which involved blowing a fantasy bubble with imaginary bubble gum, and then climbing inside it. It was the actor who had played the bully, and she was astonished to see now that he was smaller and lighter than Hal. It was a tribute to the professional skills of both that during the previous mime the opposite had appeared to be true.

Several children were picked from the audience by Hal and his companion to take part in the mime. Timmy was among them. He clung to Hal's hand with an expression of ecstatic hero-worship on his small face.

Once the series of short improvisations had finished, swarms of children clamoured for autographs. Nina, hoping to slip out unnoticed, found Tim in the midst of a crowd of envious friends—Hal had known him by name! She extracted him from the group, and made for the door.

'Did you see it?' he was demanding excitedly. 'And the way the bubble gum went splat all over his face!'

'I certainly did!' she laughed. 'And perhaps you can show me again when we get home?'

'Oh, do we have to go now?' he pleaded. 'Can't we see Hal?'

Talking to Hal just now was something she wanted to avoid. She needed time to reflect on what she had just seen. 'We've got to get home before the traffic starts,' she replied quickly—but not quite quickly enough.

'Coward,' he said in her ear, and his beard brushed against her cheek and hair. He was standing just behind her. She took a deep breath, needles pricking an awareness of him down the length of her spine, and turned to face him. 'Enjoy it?'

'Very much, thank you.' She gave a vague smile, which was the best she could manage. 'Tim certainly did. Thank you for picking him out—it's made his year, I should think.'

Hal patted Tim on the shoulder. He had to bend to reach him. 'Well done!' he enthused. 'Ever thought of being an actor?'

Tim's face shone. 'Oh, *yes*!' he breathed.

Hal never gave the slightest sign that he took the six-year-old anything but seriously, and Nina found herself admiring his unexpected sensitivity to the world of a child. In the past he would have lacked that perception.

'That's great,' he said. And then, looking straight at her, 'Well, are you coming to the play tonight? Or have you thought up some plausible excuses?' His voice was perfectly pleasant, but his dark eyes challenged her.

'Perhaps,' she said ambiguously, and then looked down at Tim. 'Come on, it's time to go.'

Hal's attention was claimed at that moment, and she got away, dragging a protesting Timmy behind her, aware that from her point of view at least the encounter hadn't been without its disturbing aspects.

Although she didn't go to *The White Devil* that night and she escaped seeing Hal in the flesh, he was just as much with her as if she had gone to the play. She couldn't help dwelling on the image of him that afternoon: the way he had kept the children spellbound. It wasn't just his voice—it was the magnetism of the personality that came through that could hold an audience. And he was talking of giving up acting! He had been destined to be an actor from the day he was born. She couldn't believe he would ever be happy doing anything else.

The following morning she was in the office with Ed, typing a letter, when he suddenly clutched his head dramatically. 'Aaargh!'

She glanced up. 'Don't do that—you gave me a fright! And you're increasing our expenditure on correcting fluid.' Carefully she began to paint over a typing error. 'And it's no good going on at me again about using the computer—it lost two entries the other day.'

'You mean you lost them. You just pressed the wrong key, that's all. You're losing your grip, old girl.'

You never said a truer word! she thought to herself grimly. I won't have any grip left if those wretched actors don't pack up and go soon. Or one wretched actor in particular. Ever since that dinner with Hal, she seemed to be living at cross purposes—one moment half hopeful that she'd see him, and the next convinced that she was courting disaster by letting him even talk to her. They couldn't safely resume any part of their old relationship, so it would be better not to see him at all. He'd already broken through some of her defences—and keeping him at arm's length was going to prove more and more difficult. She could only do it by hiding her true reactions from him, and to a certain extent from herself—it was an increasingly bad idea to examine her feelings in any way.

'So what have you done to provoke that terrible howl a minute ago?' She tried to drag her thoughts back once again to the real world of students, and language schools.

'I forgot to send those tutors' sherry party invitations.'

'Ed!' She picked up the first suitable object that

came to hand—a large and lurid eraser—and threw it at him. It bounced off his head in a very satisfying manner.

But there was no real crisis. At her insistence a programme for the academic year had been sent round at the beginning of September; once-a-term sherry parties were a virtual fixture as an attempt to establish more personal links with the tutors, whose contact with the agency was normally only by phone.

'It's this Sunday,' Ed confessed gloomily. 'I suppose I'd better start ringing up to find out if anyone read your programme for the term. . .'

'Yes, I suppose you'd better!' Nina commented unhelpfully, and went on with her own work—Ed was too good at letting her sort out confusions of his own making.

So it was she who answered the door, still grinning from one of their sillier exchanges.

Hal stood outside in drizzling rain.

'Don't you have an umbrella?' she asked, before she remembered that he was the last person it was a good idea to see, and the grin faded.

'It was fine when I started out.' There was a sheen of moisture over his dark hair and the shoulders of his leather jacket. 'Aren't you going to ask me in?'

'I'm working.'

'And I'm looking for a Japanese tutor.'

'You tried that approach the other day.'

There was an irritated shout from Ed. 'It's cold in here, Nina. Either shut the door or turn on the central heating!'

She couldn't quite assess the look Hal gave her at the sound of Ed's voice, but she said reluctantly, 'You'd better come in.'

She was going to ask him into the front room with

its formal chairs and tables. It would certainly make the point that she didn't welcome his visit, but Ed called her into the office, and Hal followed.

'Where's Julie Forman's address? She's not in the book and I can't find her in our files either. Oh, hello——' Ed's last comment was addressed to Hal, 'Is this business or social?'

Reluctantly, Nina was forced to introduce them. 'Ed Averill—Hal Crayle. Ed's my partner.' And then, 'Hal and I used to know each other.'

'Ah!' said Ed, with more enthusiasm than she had heard from him in weeks. 'My son's mystery hero!'

The two men shook hands, and it was clear that they took an instant liking to each other. Hal propped himself against Nina's desk, while they discussed vaguely his reasons for being in Cambridge, and her partner's prospects for expanding the agency. Nina, trying to pay as little attention as possible to Hal, searched for the missing address. The relevant file was in her desk—she had been checking details. Ignoring Hal, she apologised to Ed and tossed it across to him.

'We've had a slight hiatus here,' Ed explained. 'Just a little technical problem with the tutors' sherry.'

'No sherry?' Hal enquired with a grin, and that characteristic lift of one dark eyebrow.

'No tutors.'

She wasn't sure how it happened, but before long Hal was comfortably seated in an armchair, and part of the office gossip. He had also been invited to Sunday's sherry party.

'You'll certainly liven it up!' Ed enthused. 'Some of these "do"s are deadly. Even Tim's electronic spider failed to improve things last time.'

'They're not meant to be lively!' she protested, with

a warning look at him. She hadn't wanted him to invite Hal.

'Don't sound like such an old stick-in-the-mud, Nina. You're more than welcome, Hal. You might even succeed in cheering up that Miserable Minnie over there—she's had some particularly glum spells lately.'

'You speak for yourself!' she retorted, with more animation than she'd shown since Hal had arrived. 'Who's been moaning for weeks about the hazards of being self-employed?' Ed laughed, but she was aware of Hal watching her.

Ed took over the conversation for a while, pleased to have an excuse to put off the telephoning, and, with Hal lounging opposite her, his eyes on her, she found it almost impossible to put on any convincing show of work. His attention seemed to be on her business partner, and his replies were amusing and informative, but she knew that if she raised her eyes from the typewriter she would find him studying her.

Then Ed suggested, 'What about coffee? Will you make it, or shall I?'

She was grateful for an excuse to get out of Hal's range, even if it meant that he would be staying a while longer.

'I will,' she said quickly. 'Hal wants a Japanese tutor—see if you can find him one!'

Hal smiled, with characteristic lazy charm, and got to his feet in one graceful movement. 'I came to see Nina, but there's no getting inside the door without some plausible excuse. I'll help her make the coffee.'

She was about to protest, but got no support from Ed. 'Excellent idea—two coffee spoons being better than one, and all that. It's time you two stopped distracting me.'

Hal waited until they were in the kitchen before he said, 'You didn't go to the play last night.' He must have checked where her seat was.

'No.'

'Why not? It's had good reviews.'

'I told you in the summer I wasn't keen on the theatre any more.' She hated to sound so ungracious, but she couldn't afford to give an inch. She watched the kettle, willing it to boil so that she could get back to the office and be safe from this sort of conversation.

The silence that followed wasn't so much a silence as a well-calculated dramatic pause.

'I didn't get that impression when you were watching those mimes yesterday.'

'How could you tell?' she demanded, defensively. 'You were in them!'

He gave a half-smile. 'I saw you—I liked that eye-catching jersey you were wearing.'

She tried another defence. 'You're entertainers. I was entertained. Along with a couple of hundred kids and their mothers. The whole thing was very well done, but you can't take my view on that as evidence for my desire to be harrowed by nasty revenge tragedies.'

'Then come to the Greek play we're doing after *Hamlet*.'

'That's probably just as miserable.'

'So your main objection seems to be that you don't want to be miserable?' he pursued relentlessly.

'No, I don't,' she replied curtly. 'Life's bad enough without looking for what's dismal and depressing.'

He was leaning casually against the fridge, arms folded, watching her. 'Your own house in Cambridge, your own business, holidays in Greece, sherry parties—what's miserable about it, Nina?'

For a second her eyes were wary, and then she deliberately assumed that blank, shuttered look again. 'Oh,' she said flippantly. 'The sherry parties are all for tutors, not for friends.'

'Now I'm coming, too, it ought to correct that deficiency.'

'Yes,' she said coldly. 'Isn't that nice? Excuse me. I want to get the milk out of the fridge.' He moved aside, but she took care not to let her body brush his. She could tell by his expression that he had noticed.

He waited until she had put down the milk. Then he gripped her arms, forcing her round to face him. 'I'm here for just over another week,' he said quietly—but the quietness was almost a threat, and his fingers were biting into her flesh. 'You can be as cold and distant as you bloody well like, but you aren't going to stop me from trying.'

She stared at him, her lips parted in apprehension. She had been unprepared for the sudden change in him. But he wasn't going to wait for a reply. 'And before you say "nothing" in that aggravating way of yours, and try to shut me out yet again, I'd like to know what it is I'm supposed to have done. Just when I'm starting to believe that you're behaving like a rational being, and we're getting somewhere, you turn into a sort of brick wall and no matter what I do I can't get past it! And I'm beginning to be tired of trying the civilised ways of getting through to you. You know you've been a part of my life whether I liked it or not ever since you left—I told you that last summer. Why can't we at least be friends, even if we can't be anything else?'

'Hal, let me go—please. You're hurting me!' Her body was reacting to him, confusing her. It told her with devastating clarity that she wanted to be in his arms, no matter how unwise that might be. And she was sure she had only to make a move towards him for it to happen—though what the consequences might be she couldn't foresee. His hold on her didn't slacken, and she went on, rather desperately, 'We are friends—as much as we can be. . .'

'Then why won't you answer my questions? I've told you what's wrong with my life. Why won't you be honest with me about yours?'

'We can't go back to the past, Hal,' she said unsteadily. 'And even if we could, we could never just have the good bits—before it all went wrong!'

'Before *what* went wrong?' The words came out with a suppressed force that she found unnerving. 'You've never told me exactly why you walked out of my life—it was a topic you spent your time running away from last summer, if I remember rightly!'

She didn't answer immediately, but the grip on her wrists didn't slacken and the burning look in his eyes seemed to scorch her with a dark fire. In the end she couldn't bear it any longer.

'You ran my life, Hal!' she began at last, her voice accusing. 'You wanted your future no matter what the cost. Didn't it ever occur to you that you were making demands on me that I mightn't want—mightn't be able—to live up to? Once I met you I didn't even have an identity of my own! You hated my parents, and after we left Oxford I didn't even see my friends any more. Yes, I did it because I loved you, but I've often wondered since if you really loved me! Don't you think that somewhere in all that might be a reason why I left you?'

He stared at her, for the first time saying nothing. She took a deep breath to calm herself. If she wasn't careful she'd get hysterical and reveal more than she meant to. 'I don't want to talk about it any more.'

'All right,' he said slowly. She could tell nothing of his reaction from his voice. 'So what about the future?'

'I told you that, too—there can't be a future for us, not together. . .' She might have known she would have to face this discussion in the end. 'We've got totally separate lives now, Hal. You were ambitious, and you've got whatever it is you wanted——'

'I thought I'd explained about that,' he said harshly, 'or is it part of your defence against me not to listen? Don't you think people can change over five years? But I've told you why there's something missing in my life. What's wrong with yours? You still haven't answered my original question. Why aren't you happy with it?'

'I am!'

His reply was very low, but there was a quality in it now that she recognised from the old Hal—underneath all that actor's control he was furious. 'Don't lie to me, Nina—you might be able to hide a lot of things, but I know when you're not telling the truth!'

'Can't you see that everything's different now? You don't even know what I'm like any more!' Her voice began to rise, but she didn't care if Ed could hear them in the office. 'You think you want me because you remember the past differently from the way I do—but nothing's the same. It's all changed!'

She tried to pull away from him abruptly, but his grip on her only shifted to her wrists, and he grasped both in one hand to crush her close against him, one arm round her waist. 'Then I'll show you one thing that damn well hasn't!'

She guessed immediately what he was going to do and her instinct was to fight him, and to protest—but just too late. A second later his mouth came down hard on hers, and after the first contact she was horrified to feel her body flood with a response she had wanted to forget. Panic told her to pull away, and desire prompted her to cleave to him as though she were drowning.

There was no tenderness in his kiss—just anger and frustration. He took what he had wanted with a savage thoroughness, but she did nothing to prevent him, an overwhelming sense of weakness already invading her limbs. But he broke off as suddenly as he had begun, his breathing quick and uneven. And if he hadn't still held her she would have stumbled back from him and fallen.

She couldn't look at him, humiliated by the knowledge that he must have been aware of that treacherous response in her. She stared, instead, at the strong fingers circling her wrists, and wondered what she could say. There was a long silence.

His voice when he spoke was light and controlled, and utterly deadly. 'If I didn't know that behind all those defences you keep putting up—cold-bitch mask included—there was someone I very much wanted,' he said, 'I wouldn't be bothering with this. But there don't seem to be too many ways to reach you.'

He released her then, very abruptly, and, before she could even begin to think about how she could reply, he had left the room. She heard, moments later, the low, deep tones of his voice in conversation with Ed.

At first, she was too stunned to do anything—her mind numb, and her body still reacting from the effects his unexpected assault had caused in her. Then she started, slowly, to make the coffee.

CHAPTER SIX

HAL stayed until lunchtime, talking to Ed, and then at the latter's suggestion the three of them went to a local pub. In Ed's company, Nina could find no reasonable objection to being with Hal, and to have refused to go along would merely have invited her partner's comments later.

After what had just happened, she would rather have stayed alone in the house. She needed time to find a new way of coping with him, but after her subdued reappearance from the kitchen he treated her as though nothing had happened between them, making it easier to react normally to him.

But later she was glad she had had an opportunity to see him with some of his colleagues, and to learn more of him from them. She was slowly being forced to see him in a different light, and she had to admit that she had been reluctant to change that old version of the ambitious and rather insensitive young man who had ruined a part of her life. It was easier to cling to the resentment rather than to be forced to accept that her future might have been different, and that maybe in some ways she had misjudged him.

It was one of the few town pubs with a real wood fire, and the atmosphere was cosy and relaxed. One or two people looked sharply at Hal when he came in, but he chose a corner away from the windows, and did nothing to draw attention to himself.

'Why aren't you at a rehearsal?' Nina asked him

after a while. 'You seem to have a surprising amount of time to go visiting.'

'I'm not doing any more work with the company once my contract runs out after Christmas.'

'Then you really have decided to give up acting?'

'What!' It was Ed. 'Give up just when you're so successful? You must be mad.'

Hal stared into the mug of beer in front of him. 'I know what I don't want in life,' he said shortly. 'And if acting is the fastest road to what I don't want, then I'm giving up acting.' There was a silence while he looked at Nina. She met his eyes, and then glanced away. Ed was watching them.

But there was no further mention of the topic when a couple of other members of the company came into the pub, and joined them. Nina recognised Nick, one of the team she'd seen at Tim's school. He had a thin, lively face and used his hands expressively when he talked. The other was an older man with a quiet sense of humour, introduced to her as Don.

'He's had the best reviews of any of us in *Hamlet*,' Hal commented.

Don gave a quiet laugh. 'Rubbish. Are you coming to see Hal's *Hamlet*, Nina? Must be one of the first black-bearded princes of Denmark in history.'

'I always thought that Hamlet was supposed to be a blond Scandinavian with a funereal taste in clothes,' Ed said.

Nick laughed. 'He's got the undertaker's suit all right—it's just the rest of him that's a bit of a shock. I should think any genuine Danes in the audience must be scandalised.'

'Careful what you say about Hamlet's countrymen——' Hal warned. 'Nina's half Danish!'

'I thought there must be some suitably romantic

explanation for that beautiful hair,' Don remarked, with conscious gallantry. 'So how do you feel about this black-bearded pirate posing as your famous prince, and being reviewed as the "Hamlet of the century"?'

Hal looked directly across at her. 'Nina doesn't read the crits. She's not interested in the theatre.' His eyes held a direct challenge.

There was an awkward pause, but then a remark from Nick diverted the conversation into easier channels, and later he mentioned their drama work at the school, while the other three were involved in a separate discussion.

'It's true I don't go to the theatre much,' Nina admitted, 'but I did enjoy your entertainments with the children. Do you run those Drama Afternoons in every town you visit? You must be exhausted when it comes to the evening performances.'

'We take the school visits in turns. Most of us don't do them very often—though I tend to get involved in quite a few. I like working with kids. It's Hal who never gets the time off. He's our star story-teller—a real Pied Piper when it comes to children.'

She looked across at Hal, apparently absorbed in conversation. A 'Pied Piper'. . .it wasn't something that she'd seen in him five years ago, but now it wasn't so difficult to believe. Perhaps he had changed—much more than she'd realised.

She didn't see him again until the haphazardly organised party on Sunday. They had ended up with sixteen guests, not including Jenny and Hal, which were as many as could be comfortably entertained in the house. Both sitting-rooms were in use, but even so people tended to spill over into the office and back of the house.

Hal arrived late, and Ed let him in. He wasted no

time in making his way into the kitchen, where Nina was having an animated conversation with a retired schoolmistress who tutored students of Russian for her.

'This sounds fascinating,' Hal said, smiling with the kind of charm that could win an entire audience. 'Sorry to interrupt. Apologies for being so late, Nina, but Saturday nights are notorious in my profession.'

He was dressed casually in dark trousers and open-necked shirt, an expensive cashmere sweater slung round his shoulders. Nina's heart seemed to give an irregular little skip. It was impossible to meet him without being aware each time of the chemistry that was between them.

She tried to pull herself together, and then succeeded in introducing her two guests the wrong way round. But at least Ellen wasn't the kind of person to take offence. 'Hal's an actor,' she said quickly. They shook hands, Hal amused by Ellen's confused apologies for not quite knowing why she should recognise him.

Then, to her annoyance, he kissed Nina's cheek. She tried to tell herself that that was the way actors greeted everyone they knew, but it didn't help—she was remembering too vividly that last time he had kissed her.

He must have seen her expression change. 'That's an apology,' he said in her ear, just loud enough for her to catch the words.

'What for?'

'What happened last time I was here. We haven't had a chance to talk since then. Are we still friends?'

'As much as we ever were!' Her reply was deliberately ambiguous. Then she thought better of it, and softened the possible insult with a smile.

They didn't speak again for a while, but she found herself too often watching him. His height and dark looks made him remarkable wherever he was, but there was nothing of the flamboyant actor in his manner. He had a kind of quiet power that drew people to him.

By about half-past one most of the tutors had drifted away, and she had already fed a bored Timmy once with sandwiches and Coke. She was expecting Jenny and Ed to stay for lunch—the usual conclusion to a sherry party—and had shopped for the ingredients of a salad, with pâté and a quiche made in a local bakery. There had been no time to cook anything.

There was plenty for another guest, and she wondered if Hal would go or stay. She knew that she was just making things worse for herself in the long run by having him around, but she couldn't help hoping that he wouldn't leave with the others. He came back into the kitchen as she was finding another can of Coke for Tim.

'Would you like to stay for lunch?' she asked, studiously examining the contents of the fridge.

He wasn't going to let her get away with that. 'Are you asking me because you feel you have to, or because you want to?'

Why was he always trying to get some sort of declaration out of her? She met his eyes with a newly kindled hostility in her own. 'Whether you accept or refuse is up to you!'

'No. It's up to you. If you're merely asking out of politeness, I'd rather go. If you'd like me to stay, then I'd like to accept.'

What was she supposed to say? Against her better judgement, she *did* want him to stay. Why couldn't he have given her an answer without making an issue of it?

'All right—I wasn't just asking out of politeness. I know Jenny would like to meet you properly.' It happened to be true, but she knew it was a compromise.

Knowing it too, he grinned at her, then took her chin between finger and thumb and forced her to meet his eyes. 'Well,' he said, 'that *is* progess!'

She turned her head away quickly. Give him an inch, and he took about two miles!

But the rest of the afternoon was relaxed, and, perhaps because she never had to find herself in conversation with him alone, the renewed tension between them ebbed away. Later, when there was a consensus of opinion that they should move on to the Averills' for supper, Jenny was clearly enthusiastic about Hal's remaining with them. She was completely charmed by him.

Nina loved Jenny's house: it somehow represented to her everything that was missing in her own life. There was a comfortable untidiness about the large Victorian rooms, and a strong sense of the family who lived in them. Even the furniture had a welcoming look.

Nina had spent two Christmases in that house—the other years she had gone to her father in Denmark and had felt like a guest and a stranger, despite the family tie. With Ed and Jenny she felt at home.

Now she helped Jenny prepare a pasta supper in the kitchen, while Ed struggled with the sitting-room fire.

'It's a beast to light, but wonderful when it gets going,' Jenny commented. 'Perhaps Hal will have some ideas.'

Nina said without thinking, 'He always was fairly practical.'

'So!' Jenny turned to her triumphantly. 'I knew there must be some mysterious past between you two! You haven't only just met, have you? Come on—I'm dying to know. Who is he?'

'An actor with that new theatre company.'

'I know that!' her friend exclaimed impatiently. 'I've been talking to him all afternoon! He'd hardly say one word, though, about why, where or when he knew you. He's absolutely gorgeous—and obviously very interested in you. For goodness' sake, don't waste him!'

Nina concentrated on stripping the papery skins off a little heap of onions in front of her, wondering how much to say. I knew him years ago, before he was successful. We were students at the same time.'

'An old flame?'

'Something like that.'

'Why haven't we met him before?' Typically, Jenny was full of eager curiosity. 'You've been very quiet about him all this time. And there was I worrying about you being so obsessed with your work that you never had any fun! You haven't even been out for a drink with anyone for months. I thought for a while that there might be something going on with Tom Hunter. . .' She left the sentence as something between a statement and a question, and Nina felt obliged to fill in the pause. It was easier to talk about Tom than Hal.

'We had a few friendly drinks together, that's all. And to be honest I knew that he was interested, but somehow. . .well, I just didn't want to get emotionally involved——' With him, or anyone, she added to herself, and then tried to turn it into a joke. 'Good lord, the man works for me!'

'So what? He's on your books as a tutor, that's all. I noticed he wasn't at drinks today. Got the brush-off?'

'Will you stop it, Jenny?' Nina was forced to laugh. 'I haven't seen him for months—and anyway, he's off on some sort of trip to Australia in December.'

'Then it's high time you took a more positive interest in the gorgeous Hal. What more can you ask for? He's devastatingly attractive, he's got the most beautiful, sexy voice I've ever heard, he's charming, interested in other people, isn't the least spoilt by success—and he's obviously wonderful with kids, if our little hero-worshipper is anything to go by!' She took a deep breath. 'So what are you waiting for?'

Nina stared at the onions. If she peeled any more, they'd be using them into next year.

She couldn't make up her mind—she'd never spoken to anyone before of her previous involvement with Hal. But what had happened between them recently had opened, despite her, some of those doors she had so firmly shut.

Treacherously, her memory conjured up one of those scenes she'd tried hard to forget—herself and Hal engaged in one of their full-blown, theatrical rows. They'd been in the flat they had shared during their third year at Oxford. She saw herself standing on the bed, furiously angry and trying to dominate him.

'Sometimes I absolutely hate you!' she'd shouted at him, and Hal, dark eyes flashing, had shouted back some impassioned accusation—she couldn't remember any longer what they'd been rowing about. Then he'd jumped at her, and they'd both crashed down on the bed and she'd cried, not very convincingly, saying he'd hurt her. Hal had gone on pretending he was angry until laughter had overcome both of them, and whatever it was that had set them off hadn't mattered any more.

But that had been while they were both still students. After that, the rows had seemed just as theatrical outwardly, but for her they had become increasingly disturbing once she had begun to realise that Hal was taking for granted the way her future plans would have to depend on his.

'There's not much to tell about him,' she said at last. 'We lived together for two years. At the beginning I thought it was heaven. At the end it was hell.'

'What happened? Did he walk out on you?'

'No. It wasn't like that. But he doesn't seem to have seen the end as final. Or maybe he's just bored now, and wants to pick up where he thinks he left off.' She was feeling too confused just now to be fair to him—and she knew it. But she didn't yet know whether she dared put any faith in the new, rather different Hal she had seen since his arrival in Cambridge.

Jenny was undeterred. 'He doesn't strike me as the kind of man who wants to play around.'

Nina looked at her thoughtfully. 'Jen—he's an actor. He always has been. He can be whatever kind of man he wants to appear for however long it suits him.'

'Come on! Nobody can keep up an act forever! You think he's totally insincere?'

'No. . .' she said hesitantly, 'though I did suspect it at first. I'm not sure what to think any more, but I can't help wondering how well he knows himself. He says he wants to give up acting—but it's been his whole life up to now! How could he be happy without it? And when he says he wants me, I wonder about that too. . . Physically, he does—but then it's always been like that between us, and if all either of us wanted was a few hours in bed from time to time things wouldn't be this complicated. But how well can he know me as a person now, when there were things he never even guessed about me when he lived with me five years ago?'

'So why did you split up?'

She took a deep breath. 'Something happened. . .something he still doesn't know about. . .that made it impossible to stay together——'

She stopped abruptly. Suddenly she couldn't trust herself to go on. Her emotions these days were far too near the surface. Without warning, the consequences of seeing Hal over the last few days had become clear to her. If she admitted she needed him, then losing him this time would be far worse than before. And lose him she would—because, if she didn't tell him about that hidden past, then the silence, like a lie, would always be between them. She knew that her fear that the truth would split them forever was also the measure of how much, in just a few days, he had come to mean to her again.

She reached for a piece of kitchen towel to blow her nose, trying desperately to think of nothing—to empty her mind of the images that filled it.

'I'm sorry—it's the onions. . . They always do this to me.' She didn't know whether Jenny believed the excuse or not, but her friend knew when to change the subject.

Hal walked part of the way home with her soon after midnight. She had taken her bicycle with her, to ensure that she would be going home alone, but Hal, who had walked to her house earlier and had accepted a lift from Ed later on, seemed determined not to lose her company.

After the talk with Jenny she had felt unaccountably

drained of all energy, and a strange sense of unreality had possessed her. She had remained apart from much of the conversation that had been going on between the other three, and Hal, for some reason, had no longer tried to provoke her. Ed had made one remark. 'You're very silent, Nina. Worn out by this morning's socialising?' She'd seen the surreptitious dig in the ribs he'd got from Jenny, but Hal, though aware of what was going on, had never even looked at her.

Now he said little as they walked along, merely insisting on pushing her bicycle for her, holding it by the saddle and steering by touch. The air was very cold, almost frosty. Street lighting blotted out all but the brightest stars.

Hal commented once or twice on the pattern of the streets they were following, and she gave monosyllabic replies, pushing her hands deep into her pockets. She'd forgotten her gloves at Jenny's.

'Ed says that you're having a struggle with the finances of the agency.'

It was a topic that had already come up. 'I don't think it's anything serious,' she replied quietly.

'What will you do if he decides to pull out?'

That was something they hadn't talked about. 'I don't really know. I hadn't thought about it.' Still preoccupied by the thoughts she had had earlier, she would answer whatever he asked. It was too much effort to do anything else.

'They're very close friends of yours, aren't they?'

'Yes.'

Then he asked, 'Are you lonely, Nina? You want what they've got, don't you—a house that's a home, and a child? Isn't that why you spend so much time with them?'

He had told her that he wouldn't give up trying.

And all those times she had caught him watching her, he hadn't missed a thing. Now, no answer at all was the only possible reply.

'Jenny says you hardly ever go out with anyone. I don't remember you as a workaholic.'

Again she said nothing.

Hal stopped walking. They were near the town centre. She stopped mechanically. He must recognise his surroundings by now. He propped her bike against someone's railings, and then drew her under a street light. She did nothing to resist.

It was as though she had no resources left to build the barriers she had carefully maintained between them. Too often Hal had succeeded in making her react to him with a defensive anger, but there was no fight left in her now. She could only hope that he wouldn't guess at the level of her defeat, and take advantage of it. She needed time away from him to repair that mask.

Hal was looking at her, studying her face for clues, and she knew instinctively that he was resisting an urge to take her in his arms. Instead he put his hands on her shoulders. 'You're coming to the play next Saturday? No excuses this time?'

'Yes.' She was looking at him, but gave the answer almost mechanically.

'Jenny's got a ticket. You're not sitting together, but she's had strict instructions to see that you get there, and that you don't walk out before it starts.'

She gave the ghost of a smile, amused by his dictatorial manner. 'All right. What about Tim?'

'Ed's babysitting.'

'When did you arrange all this?' There seemed to have been a conspiracy between them all, and in the back of her mind she registered the way in which Hal had enlisted the help of her friends—fitting into their close little group as though he had always been part of it.

'Some time during lunch today.'

'Oh.'

He moved closer. 'Do you want me to walk the rest of the way home with you?'

She shook her head.

Then, almost as if he was risking some hostile reaction from her, tentatively he touched the side of her face with his finger, tracing the line of her cheek. He took his time, his eyes never leaving her face—though she wouldn't look at him directly—giving her plenty of time to back out if that was what she wanted to do.

She didn't know what she wanted—she was too tired to think clearly—and she didn't move. She let him put his fingers under her chin, and lift her face to him. He touched his lips to hers experimentally, but although she made no response she didn't back away. She would let him do whatever he liked. She could sense that he was already reacting to her nearness, as she was to his. There was a tension in him that told her that he would have liked to pull her even closer, but instead he brushed his mouth across hers slowly, once or twice, still holding her by the shoulders.

She began to tremble, and he slid his arms round her, holding her gently. Gradually, he teased her lips apart, kissing her in a way that she hadn't experienced since they had been together all those years ago. She let him enter her mouth, and, as that intimate exploration progressed, her own tension began to seep out of her, and she let herself relax against him.

She scarcely knew what she was doing. It seemed now to be part of the tranced state she had fallen into since earlier in the evening. She knew he wanted her, but she was also aware that he wasn't now going to try to persuade her. There was a kind of controlled gentleness about his kisses that offered her a comfort and security she found herself desperately needing. She let him deepen the kiss, but there was no sexual passion in her own response—only a kind of hopeless longing.

It was he who finally broke off, lifting his head to look down into her dazed eyes. 'Isn't this much better than fighting me?' he said softly, and then kissed the end of her nose.

She smiled at him then. 'I don't fight you all the time.'

'No,' he agreed, 'only most of it.' And then pulled her closer. He held her for a long while, his cheek against her hair, and she experienced a sense of loss as he released her.

There was nothing to be upset about. He hadn't taken any advantage of her this time; he had let her know what he was going to do, and it was she, not he, who would have prolonged the kisses. So why did she feel so upset?

He watched her as, with uncertain fingers, she turned on the lamps and got on to her bicycle—she was shivering, but not entirely with cold.

Then he said, 'I'm not going to let you forget about Saturday.'

She gave him a half-smile, avoiding his eyes. She couldn't reply—she only wanted to get home where it was safe, and quiet, and she could think about what had happened.

If he had insisted on coming home with her she wouldn't have argued, she reflected later. And if he had taken her up to bed and held her in his arms all night she would have welcomed it—and then felt a heavy sense of guilt afterwards because she had somehow taken advantage of the fact that he had wanted her, while she could give so little in return.

CHAPTER SEVEN

For most of the following week she was still moving, half-tranced, through the routine of work. Outwardly she was calm and efficient, but nothing seemed real to her. She dwelt too often on that kiss under the street lamp, on Hal's gentleness, and the way he had kept his own desires so carefully controlled.

Although she hadn't consciously accepted him as part of her life again, perhaps without her seeking it—and despite all her resistance—he was already there. But once she let him break down those final barriers, and let herself be fully vulnerable to him, he would discover what it was she had been hiding and find it too hard to accept. She would hurt him and hurt herself, and then, after the inevitable rejection, the agony of five years ago would start all over again.

He rang twice during the first part of the week only, he said, to remind her to turn up at the play—the local reviews had been very good—but both 'reminders' turned into very long calls. She found it surprisingly easy to chat to him when he presented no immediate threat to her.

Then on Thursday he appeared on the doorstep at about twelve-thirty. 'I'm taking you out to lunch,' he announced. 'Ed can hold the fort.'

Things had somehow changed between them since that night at Ed and Jenny's. She was more pleased to see him than she would have believed a week ago—but she couldn't afford to show it too openly.

He was watching her as she came down to the hall

after fetching her coat, making her feel absurdly self-conscious. He waited until she was close to him, and then took both ends of her scarf in his hands to pull her against him, looking down at her.

She gave a little gasp as she was jerked forward, and gazed up at him, lips parted, suddenly apprehensive. He smelled of a spicy cologne. She thought he was going to kiss her.

'I like that scarf—you look good in scarlet,' was all he said, and then he let her go abruptly. She was annoyed with herself for the tiny pang of disappointment, and suspected that he was aware of both the disappointment and her reaction to it. She knew that he was dividing her against herself, though how consiously he was doing it she couldn't guess. Common sense and self-preservation warned her to keep her distance, but she couldn't help dwelling on the changes she had noted in him, as much in his attitude to others as to herself.

He drove her out to a pub in one of the villages, where the food was good, and they were left undisturbed. At first he told her about the house he had bought in St Albans after making a lot of money from a film. He had scarcely found time to live in it since, but he described it in terms that made her curious to see it.

The conversation was easy and relaxed, very much in the manner of the phone calls, but after a while he said, 'I've got a decision to make. I want to ask you what you think about it.'

'Oh?' She looked wary again. If he was trying to involve her in his life, it was time to back off.

'I've been to see my partner in the electronics business. He's thinking of taking a job in the States. So that gives me three choices—either I can buy him out of the partnership and go into running the business full-time, assuming I can find a new head of research, or I can change the nature of the business, shut down the research, and concentrate on selling what we've already got.'

'Or?' she prompted.

'Or we can both sell up at a profit.'

She studied him carefully. 'What you're really talking about is giving up acting, isn't it?'

There was a pause. He was looking her directly in the eyes, his own dark eyes unreadable. 'What do you think I should do?'

'But Hal——' she protested, 'it's got nothing to do with me! I can't tell you how to make that sort of decision about your life!'

'No, but you can tell me what you think—what your reactions are.'

She stared at him, her eyes a brilliant aquamarine, full of all the emotions that she couldn't admit to openly. Then she said, 'I think you're crazy. Acting's been your life. It's what you've been obsessed with since before I knew you. You've wanted success—sometimes, I used to think, too much—and, now you're almost there, you want to chuck it all in. Why, for heaven's sake?'

'I told you that last summer.'

'Yes, but even if you do want some sort of a stable background—wife, home, family, whatever—acting doesn't have to exclude those things! It's up to you to make sure that, once you've got them, you keep them.'

He studied her in silence for a moment, the bearded, handsome pirate's face impassive. Then he said, 'OK. That's all I wanted to know.' And changed the subject.

He drove back to the house by mid-afternoon and dropped her outside. 'I'm relying on Jenny to get you to the play,' he said as they parted. 'You've got to see at least one live Crayle performance if your advice is to be any good.'

'It wasn't advice, Hal,' she said quickly. 'It was just my opinion.'

'Then you've got to have some basis for your opinion. See you.'

There was a powerful roar, and the car disappeared like a dark blue bullet. That made her smile—there was nothing ostentatious about him as a successful actor, but there was one area in which he hadn't been able to resist the dreams of his youth!

She met Jenny at the theatre on Saturday night. They exchanged notes about the working week briefly, and then Jenny said, 'I'm dying to see this. It doesn't last very long, but it's had brilliant reviews. It's a pity, though, that it's not really Hal's play—I had a look through the text, and it's the heroine who gets all the good lines.'

'I don't know it,' Nina said. 'Except that one of the tutors told me that it's rather gloomy.'

'Well, if you'd gone to the first one he gave you a ticket for, you wouldn't have had to come tonight,' Jenny said firmly. 'I suspect Hal just wants to show off to you.'

'If he does, he should know me better than that.' But she felt obliged to be fair to him, and added, 'If he'd really wanted to show off, he'd have given me a ticket for *Hamlet*.'

They were sitting nowhere near each other. Nina wasn't tempted to leave, but she wasn't looking forward to the performance either. She couldn't help but be aware that the experience of seeing Hal on the stage was something so interwoven with their past together that, inevitably, it would have associations that she would find painful. As Jenny had said, the play was short, but that was possibly its only merit. She wondered if Hal would contrive to see her afterwards.

To begin with she resigned herself merely to observing, in a detached sort of way, and caught herself looking at her watch several times. But gradually she became caught up in it.

The actors were all masked, but she would have identified Hal immediately by his voice even if she hadn't known which part he was playing from the programme. The story was extremely powerful, dealing as it did with the violent and bitter feelings of a woman towards her husband when he set her aside in favour of another.

The husband, played by Hal, seemed to be almost unfeeling towards his first wife in the way that he allowed himself to be dominated by political ambition. At first she saw little similarity between the events and characters of the play and her own life, but, as the story progressed, she found herself being caught up in it in a way she would never have guessed.

The climax of the play was the killing of her young sons by the distraught wife. In private the woman was agonised—torn two ways by love and pity for her children, and an overwhelming need to make her husband suffer—but in public she appeared calm and unmoved, masking her inner unhappiness. Nina found herself increasingly involved in the drama, and unable to bear the heightening tension. She knew what it cost to wear that mask. In a way she couldn't define, it was as though she was looking at some part of herself in that violent and passionate woman.

And she knew what it was to have to sacrifice a child.

A terrible guilt hung over her, and it had darkened

her life for five long years. She had had a child—Hal's child—and she had never even given him a chance to fight for what was his. She had turned to her parents, even agreeing in the end to give up the baby for adoption, worn down by her mother's arguments and tears. The child had been premature, and, after a difficult birth, had struggled for only a few hours of life. She had tried to comfort herself afterwards with the thought that, had her little son lived, she would have defied her parents no matter what the cost and nothing on earth would have made her give him up.

But the cold, hard reality was the fact that before the birth she had agreed to do what her mother wanted—to hand him over for adoption—because to keep him, it seemed, would ruin either Hal's life, or her own.

She no longer saw the masked actress on the stage, but herself, as she had been over five years ago when she had tried to tell Hal she was having his child.

She had known she was pregnant for weeks. Her initial reaction—half fright, half delight—had darkened over those weeks as the doubts had grown. She had wanted to share her news instantly, but Hal had been continually preoccupied; they had been moving from one financial crisis to the next, so that the right moment had never seemed to come.

She had always assumed that they would marry, even though they had never actually discussed it, but confronted with the reality of an ill-timed pregnancy—unwanted as far as Hal was concerned—she had begun to question their relationship. He had said he loved her, and had even seemed to take for granted that she would always be there for him, but he surely wouldn't want to marry her when his career was at its most precarious. . . It might ruin his future to get tied up with a wife and child so soon. And he had been desperately ambitious.

She remembered the last night she had ever spent with him, most of it alone in the cold little bathroom that had belonged to their cheap lodgings. There had been torn linoleum on the floor, and a draught under the door. He had just returned from an unsuccessful audition and had been keyed up about a second, only days away. Obsessively, he would talk about nothing else, and there would *never* be a right moment, she had thought despairingly. She had sat down on the edge of the bath and cried, and she had never felt so desolate in her life.

They had no money; and with no money they had no future. Finally, she had decided to ask her parents for help. They didn't approve of Hal, and they would be horrified by the prospect of an illegitimate grandchild, but maybe she wouldn't have to tell them. Maybe they would lend her some money and then she and Hal could get married, and they needn't know until afterwards.

A little comforted by the decision she had made, she had decided to broach the subject again with Hal the next day. They had been sitting in a cheap café, and she remembered looking at him across the table, her heart thumping in her chest, nerving herself for the moment when she would tell him. They had been talking, and she had told him of her decision to visit her parents, trying to prepare for what she had to say. There had been a sudden brooding silence. He had been fiddling with his coffee spoon, looking tense and irritated.

There had been a couple of small children at the next table—one screaming with temper and the other crying in sympathy. The harassed tones of their mother had been audible to the entire café. Nina had watched Hal nervously. And what he had said then had changed the entire course of their relationship.

'Why the hell can't some women keep their brats quiet?' he had demanded savagely. 'Do they have to make the place torture for everyone else?' He had flicked the spoon carelessly on to the table. She could still hear it clatter on the bare wood. Then he had looked across at her. 'Some kids should be drowned at birth.'

There had been no way that she could find the courage to tell him about the baby after that.

The theatre was stifling. The blackness around her pressed in upon her, threatening to engulf her, and she could no longer bear to watch the woman on the stage. Abruptly, she got up from her seat. She was almost at the end of a row. The person sitting next to her gave a grunt of surprise then stood up, still intent on the play, to let her pass. She was out of the dark, spellbound auditorium in seconds.

Her car was in the central multi-storey not far away, and she almost ran to reach it. Inside she was in a turmoil of blind emotions, with only one overwhelming need—to get away, to get home, away from that curiously distorted portrayal of herself with the very man whose life had so shattered the pattern of hers.

She wasn't even aware of the maze of streets as she drove home, her mind fixed on the moment when she could be inside her own house, with the door shut between herself and the outside world. There she could scream, or cry, or rage out the storm inside her just as she felt it, and there'd be no one to see.

She leant back against the front door. She didn't want the light on—only the darkness could give scope to what was inside her. She didn't know what she wanted to do, and the old habit of self-control kept telling her, 'Not yet, not yet.'

She ran upstairs with almost feverish energy, and turned on the television in the sitting-room. It didn't matter what was on. Anything to fill her head with other images—harmless ones that would replace everything that was pushing to the forefront of her mind.

Pictures succeeded each other on the screen, conveying nothing to her. She had no idea how long she watched them. Inside, she was still in a whirling blackness, and terrified of looking into herself to examine any of the thoughts and feelings that threatened to engulf her. Not yet.

There was a whisky bottle on the sideboard; it was almost full. Ed had given it to her. She didn't really like it, but she poured out a whole tumblerful, and started to drink. It burned like fire and after the first couple of mouthfuls she choked and coughed, and was forced to put it down, her eyes smarting.

Perhaps if she had a bath—something to do—to delay the moment when everything would come crashing down on her. But, she thought stupidly, she had bathed before she went out. Maybe she should get into bed and drink the rest of the whisky, and then just lie there and wait for it to take effect?

She went into the bedroom and started to strip off her clothes, leaving them where they dropped. What did it matter? She could pick them up tomorrow, any time. Nothing really mattered when you thought about it. . .

She found her nightshirt, and turned back the covers of the bed. When she got in she remembered the whisky glass in the sitting-room. She climbed out again to put on a dressing-gown. It was a bit too big for her and wrapped her completely in its blue towelling folds.

Just as well. It was chilly and she hadn't turned the central heating up very high.

She went back into the sitting-room in her bare feet. Don't think—don't remember. Not yet. She took a deliberately large mouthful of whisky and swallowed it. She hadn't finished coughing when the doorbell rang. Perhaps it was Jenny. Well. There were no lights on. If it was Jenny she would try to telephone later. 'Go away,' she said pointlessly as the bell rang again.

It rang insistently. Finally it rang continuously. Damn. Her car was outside. Jenny would know she was there. Still, better Jenny than anyone else. She wondered if she smelt of whisky.

Hal was outside when she pulled the door open, leaning casually against the bell. She stared at him for a moment in disbelief. Of course it would be him! Why hadn't she guessed? Then she realised that he was still ringing.

'Stop that!' Her voice sounded husky and unreliable. 'You'll wake up everyone in the street.'

'Then ask me in or I'll ring it all night.' She could see that he was taking in her dishevelled appearance, and the fact that she was wearing a bathrobe.

She took a step back, and before she had time to think he was inside, shutting the door behind him. 'What's the matter?' he asked. He sounded concerned.

'Nothing. You woke me up,' she lied. 'Go away, Hal. I can't stand much more of this.'

'More of what, exactly? You were crying in your sleep?'

Hastily she brushed a hand across her face. There were tears on her cheek. 'I was coughing,' she said curtly.

'I see.' He studied her for a moment in the half

darkness of the hall. 'And was the whisky the cause or the remedy?'

She couldn't cope with him now—not Hal of all people. The defences were getting dangerously fragile. 'That's none of your business. Go away, Hal. I've got work to do tomorrow.' It was the first thing that came into her head.

'On *Sunday*?' he said.

If she'd wanted to get rid of him she should have shut the door straight away. She felt desperate.

'I want to talk to you.'

Unconsciously she was twisting her hands in the folds of her bathrobe.

'Why did you leave before the end of the play?'

'How do you know I did?'

'Jenny saw you. And I looked for you afterwards.'

'Where is Jenny?'

'She's gone home. Do we have to stand here?'

'I want you to go *now*,' she said, desperate. 'Please, Hal.'

'Not until you've told me why you left before the end.' He was halfway up the stairs. Helplessly she watched as he mounted them.

'I need whisky too,' he said. 'It must be something about Greek drama.'

'I felt ill,' she said, clutching at a straw. 'I feel ill now—so *please* go!'

'Then I'll look after you.' He had disappeared on to the landing. She heard a lamp switched on in the sitting-room. 'Don't you ever turn any lights on here?'

She lingered indecisively in the hall. A sense of nightmare gripped her again. None of this was really happening—maybe she had fallen asleep, and in her dream this was just a continuation of the play.

How was she going to get him to go? This wasn't a

dream, because she couldn't wake up from it. Perhaps if she screamed and cried out all those feelings that were still there, he'd leave. Screaming women on stage were one thing—she doubted whether he could handle the reality. But then. . .maybe he could, and in a way she wouldn't be able to cope in her turn. She'd *have* to get him to leave.

She went upstairs, and found him in the sitting-room. He had taken off his jacket and was wearing the standard actor's uniform of jeans and sweatshirt, this one printed with the logo 'Classical Actor's Company'. She wondered if he had any clothes on underneath. There was something about him that suggested he had dressed in a hurry.

He had a glass of whisky in his hand. It contained a quarter of the quantity hers did, standing conspicuously on a low table where she had left it.

He raised his glass to her, and took a sip. 'For medicinal purposes only.' When she didn't move, he asked, 'Aren't you going to drink yours?' and sat down on the sofa by the little table, watching her.

She picked up the glass and took a cautious sip, and then another. Perhaps if she got drunk he'd go away. She was already beginning to feel the unsteadying effects of her first couple of mouthfuls. She wished she'd had supper—her grip on what was real was weakening, and her conscious control of herself and the situation seemed to be slipping away from her. All those dark things she'd been pushing to the back of her mind since the play were threatening to escape again, but as vague, mixed-up unhappy shadows—the borderlines between loss and guilt and bitterness had blurred.

Quickly she took another large mouthful and swallowed it without thinking. While she choked for breath, and the tears stung her eyes, she was aware that Hal had taken the glass from her fingers, and was pulling her down on to the sofa beside him. She didn't have the strength to resist.

His arms were round her, and he held her until she had stopped coughing. 'How much of that did you have before I arrived?'

'Only a bit,' she said weakly, and wiped her eyes with the back of her hand.

She shouldn't be there, half sitting on his knee. She tried to rise, but he held her, apparently without effort. Her leg was half entangled through his and he had slipped a hand through the opening of her robe. She could feel the warmth of his fingers through the cotton of her nightshirt as he caressed her gently along the length of her side. But she felt strangely passive—unable to make the decision that would separate them.

Then she felt him touch her hair with his lips, and she stiffened. She knew instinctively that he had registered it.

'Why do you eat so little, and work so much, and drink half a pint of whisky to send yourself to sleep after a play?' he asked gently.

His voice was a low murmur in her ear, and his breath stirred her hair. She knew he wanted to kiss her, but she didn't know how to evade him. Already, part of her was registering the pleasant, soothing caress of his hand. It must be the whisky that was making her willing to accept it. She didn't answer.

The hand moved a little lower, on to her bare leg, and then up under her nightshirt, stroking the length of her hip and thigh. His lips touched her brow, and followed her hairline, barely making contact with her skin. His breath fanned her face. Stop—stop! she wanted to cry, but she couldn't—yet. There was somehow such comfort in it, and something she had missed for so long. His beard brushed her cheek and he kissed the side of her face. Then his fingers touched the sensitive skin beneath her breast, and followed its soft swell upwards. She went rigid, struggled to sit up. 'No, Hal—don't! I don't want you to!'

'All right—calm down, darling.' His voice was deep and quiet, and his lips were in her hair again. He moved his hand down to her waist.

Her heartbeat had quickened, and it took a long time before she relaxed a little, the tension slowly seeping out of her body. After what seemed like hours, she said, 'It's very late. I think you ought to go.'

He looked down at her, but he didn't move. 'Do you really mean that?'

About to tell him *yes*, she knew that she didn't. She wanted him to stay. But if she let him, she couldn't expect him to sit like that with her all night—only, once he had gone she would be alone, and she would have to face that darkness all over again.

When she didn't answer, he shifted his position, and leaned across her to rearrange the cushions at the end of the sofa. Then before she could move away, he had swung both her legs on to the sofa and gently pushed her back against the cushions.

He was kneeling astride her, bending down over her, his hands either side of her face. She lay staring up at him through wide eyes, magnetised by his closeness, on a knife-edge of indecision.

They seemed to look at each other for a long time, as though assessing the unknown quantity that the other presented. Then, when he moved to kiss her, lowering himself slowly on to her, she panicked. She had fought, over and over again, to keep him away, to preserve the separateness she maintained at a cost she was too proud to admit to anyone—and now because in half an hour, or however long it was, she had allowed him to regain that power over her he had always had, she was going to throw away everything.

She struggled desperately, every move making contact with some part of his body, while his strength drew her closer and closer against him, crushing her like a steel trap.

'Don't fight me, darling. I don't want to hurt you!' His mouth was close to her ear. She could feel the warmth of his breath as he drew her under him, to half imprison her with his weight.

'Let me go!' she sobbed. 'Hal, please—not like this. . .'

'Hush, sweetheart.' Every word, every caress sent her pulses racing even while she fought him. 'Stop crying. It's all right.' He soothed her as he would a frightened child, stroking her hair and her back as he held her against him, until her resistance became passive and she lay without movement, utterly unresponsive in his arms.

She couldn't tell whether it was he who had defeated her, or she who had given in. He stroked her hair, and then, when she made no movement to protest, slowly unfastened the buttons of her nightshirt, pushing back the fabric, and caressing the smooth skin of her shoulders and neck.

He was fully clothed, but the feel of his body against hers was beginning to light little fires under her skin. He eased himself back from her, his weight on one elbow propped against the cushions. He was watching her as, with one slow finger, he traced the bones of her neck, and then drew a line down one breast. As his fingertip circled it, the nipple hardened, and he bent his head to tease it with his mouth and continue the slow circling with his tongue. She dug her nails into the cushions, and bit her lip to prevent herself from betraying by any sound the thrill of pleasure that had just sparked through every nerve end.

He raised his head to look down at her again, and then said, in that slow, deep voice that was seduction in itself and had always gone right through her, 'What's the matter? You never used to be so silent. Doesn't that turn you on any more?'

'No.' The little gasp, all she could manage, was an ineffectual denial and she knew it, and, as she tried to twist under him to turn her body away from such a direct attack upon her senses, she saw him look down at her taut breasts. He touched their centres, hard and erect, with the palm of his hand, and she heard the amusement quite clearly in his voice as he murmured, 'Nina, you're a beautiful liar!' before his mouth took hers.

She made one last attempt to fight him then, tensing her muscles to resist and push him away from her if she could, but he had her too tightly locked to him, trapping her with his weight and tangling one hand in her hair to prevent her from twisting away from his kiss. But, despite the iron control he was exercising over her body, his lips were gentle, moving lightly over hers, just brushing her trembling mouth to tease it into response.

Then the rigid resistance of her limbs melted like ice under the heat of his body. She felt her loins flood with the desire she had known only in his arms. He drew away from her to quickly strip off the printed sweat-shirt and unfasten his jeans, and then pushed up the flimsy nightshirt above her breasts before lowering himself on to her again. His breathing was rapid and uneven, and he gave a groan as he let his weight sink against her, catching her face between his hands to cover her with kisses before he sought her mouth.

A little moan escaped her as his tongue slid back and forth to part her lips and as she opened them to him, almost unaware of her own response, she slipped her arms round his neck to draw him even closer and pressed her aching breasts against the rough hair of his chest.

His kiss instantly deepened, and she felt his hand slide down over the curve of her hip. He shifted his weight away from her so that she was no longer trapped under him. Dizzy with the scent and feel of him, her body sought his. For a second, he was touching her only with his mouth, and the arm under her shoulders. She writhed to get close to him again, drawn by the magnet of that heated body. His touch instantly released little spirals of pleasure inside her that wound their way through her until she groaned against his lips. She thought she would die of the unappeased hunger he had created—the hunger of five years for the man who had been her only lover—until his body slid across hers and he coupled them together.

She had forgotten what an expert lover Hal had been. He could master her body utterly, bringing her back from the verge of one ecstatic peak after another, until she could bear it no longer and heard her own voice like a stranger's begging him to release her.

As the pleasure exploded inside her, tearing through her like shock waves, she heard Hal groan and felt the tension suddenly leave him. His full weight was on her and his face was buried in the tangle of her hair. His arms slowly slid round her back to hold them in an embrace that locked them together. Her face was wet, and she found that she was weeping silently, the tears sliding from under her closed lids. She found herself stroking his hair, half murmuring, half crying, over and over again, 'Oh, my darling. . .my darling. . .' His hair was thick and silky, and a little too long. Just as she had known it would be.

He turned his face into her neck, and his beard prickled her shoulder. His voice when he spoke was unsteady and rough-edged. 'I love you, Nina.'

But she couldn't answer.

CHAPTER EIGHT

THEY lay together for a long time without speaking.

Still dazed by the intensity of the experience they had shared, Nina followed her thoughts disjointedly. . . He had told her he loved her, but, although she had responded instantly to those deceptively simple words, she couldn't stifle a small voice of doubt: what did they really mean? They were more than a statement of fact, or a confession of surrender: they were also a demand for something in return.

He wanted a home, a child, and she had already denied him both, although he didn't know it. And the stability she craved was something she doubted they could ever give each other.

For five years she had lived in limbo, a safe no man's land where nothing hurtful intruded. She had learned that ordinary life wasn't made of the dramatic peaks and chasms of Art—it was a series of gentle hills and valleys most of the time. But between her and Hal there would never be real tranquillity, however much they both wanted it. It was the way they were—they could never be an Ed and Jenny, because between them, although Hal wasn't really aware of it, there would always be the shadow of a bitter past.

His head was heavy against her shoulder, and, absently, she found herself stroking the thick, silky hair. She wanted him desperately, she could admit that to herself now, and to live without him again would be a renewed pain that she didn't know how she was going to bear. But nothing had really changed between them. He had said he loved her, but could he still say it if he knew what she had kept hidden from him?

How could I have been so stupid as to let this happen? she thought with despair. We should never have become involved with each other again. Now, one way or the other, she would have to hurt him, and be hurt herself, just as before.

She felt him stir at last, and ease himself away from her. He propped himself on one elbow and looked down on her. The expression in his eyes made her want to weep.

She put up one hand to pull down her nightshirt, but he caught it and held it. 'Don't,' he said. 'I want to look at you.' There was still an unsteady roughness in his voice—a sign of genuine emotion with none of the actor's control. . .and she had wondered if she would ever be certain of his sincerity!

Her shirt, pushed up above her breasts, covered nothing, and although her arms were through the sleeves of the bathrobe, the rest of it was crushed beneath her. He was silent, gazing at her.

'Hal——'

He smiled. His voice when he spoke now held that golden, warm tone that was a renewed seduction in itself. 'You're every bit as beautiful as I remembered from that day on the beach.' He sounded so happy that she couldn't bear it. 'Darling, I love this sofa, but don't you have a bed?'

It was now or never. 'Hal—I want you to go.'

'You mean you didn't like it?' He sounded half teasing, half incredulous. He didn't believe she was serious.

His mouth touched the corner of hers. If she let him kiss her, she was lost. She turned her head aside abruptly and tried to push him away. 'I mean it—I should never have let you do this—it was a mistake. I had too much to drink.'

He stared down at her in disbelief, his dark brows joined together in a frown. 'I don't believe I'm hearing this! Are you trying to tell me that what happened just now didn't mean anything to you?'

'Yes—yes, of course it did,' she said desperately, 'but it doesn't change anything!' She couldn't bear to see the look in his eyes.

'And you're trying to pretend that you only did it because you were *drunk*?'

'Yes—no. Hal, just go. Please.' She tried to wriggle out from under him, but his weight still trapped her.

'And I suppose it's the whisky and not me that makes you react when I do this to you?' The skilful assault of his mouth and hands that followed made her almost instantly want to give herself to him all over again.

He was no more happy than she. He believed, wrongly, that she could fill the void in his life, and she was agonisingly tempted to make believe that she could, just for a few hours, so that however briefly they could find some sort of haven in each other's arms. But that was something she couldn't afford to do, for his sake as well as hers.

After the first few moments, she resisted him, fighting to keep herself from reacting too obviously to his touch, but when he suddenly pulled away from her and sat up, allowing her to move dazedly from under him, he said, 'I think that just proved *my* point, and not yours—don't you?' He sounded angry, and she couldn't meet his eyes.

'I never denied that sex wasn't good between us!' she replied shakily. 'But sex isn't love, and we were too young before—too turned on by each other to know the difference.'

'I don't believe that was true then and it certainly isn't now—and you know it.'

He was standing beside her, fastening the waistband of his jeans, and for a second she fought the perverse desire to draw him back to her. Some part of her wanted him to sweep away all her objections, break through the resistance she could only just put up against his physical attack on her senses so that she could give in, knowing that there was nothing else she could do. But her rejection had hurt him too deeply—and not just his pride. He wouldn't try again now without some signal from her—and that she wasn't going to give.

She sat up slowly and pulled down her nightshirt. Then she wrapped the bathrobe round her defensively, and sat huddled on the sofa, not trusting herself to move in case she found herself in his arms.

'We're not good for each other, Hal. I never wanted this to start again. Too much has happened. You can't turn back the clock and just wipe out whatever went wrong in the past.'

'As I told you before, I wasn't aware anything had gone wrong until you walked out,' he said bitterly. 'Perhaps you could have tried talking—it's the way people usually communicate.' He was standing looking down at her. He seemed immensely tall, and there was a tension in his body that told her he was trying to control emotions she could only guess at.

'I did,' she said wearily, 'but there was a time when you weren't so keen to listen. We're different people now, Hal, but some things haven't changed. You'll never give up acting—and that's right. It's the air you breathe. You'd have no life without it. But it's not for me. I've made a job and a life here.' What she was telling him were half-truths, but it was the only explanation she could give—she couldn't tell him that she was trying to protect him from the very knowledge that he'd been trying so hard to get.

'So what?' he said bitterly. 'You're not happy—don't try and pretend you are.'

She shut her eyes, but she had read the pain and anger in his. She could hardly bear it. She wanted to throw her arms round him, and tell him that she loved him, and that if only he could find some way to love her that would obliterate that disastrous conclusion to their past, she would never leave him. But their lives were separate paths now. They should never have crossed.

She covered her face with one hand, and made an effort to speak calmly. 'Hal, I can't take any more of this. Please, just go.'

There was a silence that strung her nerves to breaking point, and then he spoke. She couldn't look at him, but the intensity of controlled anger in his voice was such as she had never heard before.

'Sometimes I wish to God I'd never met you,' he said, and that amazing actor's voice vibrated with a passion that could never have been mere technique. 'You've played hell with my life, Nina! You seem to think that you can take just as much as you want from me, and then walk out when and how you choose——'

'That's not fair!' The injustice of it snapped her last shreds of control. She didn't care that she was shouting at him. 'I didn't choose to walk back into it—*you* chose! I asked you—I *begged* you to leave me alone! I didn't want you or any of this!'

Her eyes had darkened with passion, burning like

Arctic ice in conflict with the fire of hurt fury they met in his. The rows in their past had been nothing to this—there was no sense of enjoying the drama of it now. Never had she seen him so angry, and never had she cared less what he might do to her—she had a weapon more terrible than any he could use. All this was his fault! She had wanted to spare him, but if he provoked her beyond bearing, she would use it, and use it to hurt as much as she knew how.

She thought that the very air between them would crackle into flames that instant. Then, abruptly, he turned on his heel. She heard him run downstairs, and the front door slammed behind him.

Then she let herself collapse on the sofa, where less than an hour ago she had known what it was to have his love. She wept as she had never wept before. Once again, her life was empty, and it was even worse than the last time.

She woke, wondering where she was. There was a cold daylight in the room, and the lamp still shone feebly. She felt cramped and ill as she levered herself awkwardly off the sofa. Her head ached like fire and her eyes stung.

She caught sight of herself in the gilt-framed mirror on the wall. All the colour had drained from her face, and with her pale tangle of hair she looked like a distraught ghost. Her eyes were shadowed, and suspiciously puffy. She pulled her fingers through her hair, and peered at the stains of tears that were still on her cheeks.

In the bathroom she splashed water on her face, and found a comb to tease carefully through the snarled strands of hair. She didn't really look much better, and she felt like death.

There was someone at the door. She could pretend she wasn't in. The bell rang again. Perhaps it was Jenny, come to see if she was all right after leaving the play last night. Last night. . . Whoever it was, they were being very persistent. It might help to see Jenny.

She went downstairs, securing the bathrobe round her. What time was it? She realised, looking at the door, that she hadn't even been down to fasten the Yale catch after Hal had slammed it. She opened it. And then stood dumbly staring.

Hal was dressed differently. He wore a dark pair of trousers, and she hadn't seen the shirt before. He wore his leather jacket. The details registered themselves separately. He looked haggard.

'We haven't finished our discussion,' he said curtly, and brushed past her into the hall. 'I'm sorry I lost my temper last night.'

It had never occurred to her for a moment that he might come back. What had happened between them had seemed so final. She sighed. A strange calm had entered her now. A turmoil of emotions had been wept out in that storm last night after he had gone. She believed that there was nothing left in her.

'Hal. We've said everything. There's no point in prolonging this.' She was surprised at how distant her voice sounded. Her head was throbbing.

He was examining her critically. 'You should have let me stay with you last night. We might both have got some rest in the end.'

'Please go, Hal.'

'No. I've come to breakfast. Nick's just dropped me, and he's borrowing my car for a few hours. He's picking me up at lunchtime, and we have to be in Manchester by this afternoon. I've got about three hours to find out what I want to know.' He looked grim and determined, and knew only too well how to use his height as a threat. 'So you're going to tell me.'

She looked at him in silence. 'Very well,' she said quietly. 'First I'm going to get dressed.'

Taking her time, she cleared up her clothes from the bedroom floor where she had strewn them the night before, then she ran a bath and got into it, carefully keeping her mind from all thought of the conversation that would follow. By the time she was dressed, she looked exactly as she did every day for work: smart, detached, and businesslike. She couldn't afford the slightest trace of that wild, half-dressed creature Hal had seen last night. It was too strong a reminder of what had once been.

When she came downstairs there was a smell of toast and coffee, and Hal was sitting at the kitchen table, a Sunday supplement propped in front of him. He must have found the papers in the porch while she was upstairs.

He took in the significance of her appearance at first glance. 'I hope that aggressive outfit is as bullet-proof as it looks. I get to choose the weapons this time.' And then, 'Dressed like that you remind me of your mother.'

He hadn't wasted any time in opening the attack. Yes, he could hurt her, despite all that indifference she had found since last night, but she had a weapon far more wounding than he suspected, and, if he pushed her too far, she might just use it. It was one way of putting an effective end to everything.

She turned away to get the milk and butter from the fridge, her face blank. He had more or less laid the table. Then she took the cereal packets from beside the bread-bin, and the bowls from the china cupboard.

She never forgot that terrible morning. They began

calmly, polite to each other, remarking on the Sunday front-page news like any normal couple at breakfast. She drank her coffee, and passed him the milk, and the butter, and nibbled a piece of toast until he had finished eating, and then cleared the table. All the time, underneath, she was aware of the rapidity of her heartbeat that told her she was about to face an inquisition.

She stacked the dirty plates on the draining-board mechanically, and put back some of the food in the fridge. She was about to wash up, when he said, 'Leave that. Sit down.'

Obediently, she sat opposite him, her hands on the table. She didn't try to avoid his eyes, but met them fully, careful to reveal nothing in her own.

He said, 'I've wasted a lot of time wondering how to reach you, Nina. Last night I thought I'd made it. One thing I'd like to know—just for the record if nothing else—did I succeed, for even one small part of a second, in getting through any of that complex system of swinging doors that passes as your mind? I'm tired of finding that just as one opens, another slams in my face.'

She looked at him without reaction. 'Yes,' she said. It was the only answer she could give, but it was obvious that she didn't intend to explain further.

He took a deep breath, and released it slowly. Then he leaned back casually, balancing himself on the back legs of his chair. His voice when he spoke was, as usual, deep and pleasant, and she was totally unprepared for the impact of his words.

'You know, Nina, when I see you sitting there like that, with your eyes blank, and your face a beautiful mask, I want to hit you.'

It was the control with which he spoke that made

the words so deadly. She blinked, flinching a little as though he had struck her.

He saw that his words had had the desired effect, and looked down, the side of his mouth quirking in a grim smile. 'I've never hit a woman yet—except on stage—so you needn't worry.'

No. The way he could use his voice, he didn't have to.

There was another pause. Then he asked, 'Again, strictly for the record. . .why *did* you leave me?'

So there it was again—the question she had been refusing to answer ever since chance had brought them together months ago on a Greek island. In the last few days, she had faced this moment too often in her imagination to be upset by it.

There wasn't much point in lying, or refusing to answer, or wrapping it up any other way. The sooner she told him, the sooner they could put an end to this. 'I was pregnant,' she said.

There was a thunderous silence. His face showed absolutely nothing.

'I see,' he said, after what seemed a lifetime. 'Wasn't it mine?'

That did get some reaction out of her. The deliberate cruelty of the question cut her deeply, but her reflex was to return the attack. The aquamarine eyes sparked dangerously. 'How many lovers do you imagine I had time for all the while you were so busy acting?'

Again his voice was devastatingly pleasant. 'I've no idea. It's just that I'd have thought you might have told me if I was going to be a father, that's all.'

She stared at him without speaking. A muscle twitched in his cheek, but, apart from the calculated hurt in his reply, there was no other sign that what she had said had made much impact on him at all.

'Why didn't you tell me?'

Because you never gave me the chance. Because I didn't want to spoil your life. And because you didn't seem to care anyway, she thought miserably. But she said nothing.

'Nina!' His grip on her wrist was like a vice. His fingers bit deep into her flesh, almost crushing her bones. She gasped, and tried ineffectively to pull free.

It was a warning. She might think she could hurt him more than he could hurt her, but he wasn't going to let her get away unscathed. And she was doing something she never thought she would do—using a piece of knowledge she'd intended to protect him from as a weapon to wound.

Why was it that they could still do this to each other? She had believed, mistakenly, that last night had drained her of everything. No one she'd ever known could push her to that limit—and then some more.

'Do you really think I didn't try?' she asked then, her voice hard. 'My God, Hal, you were the most arrogant monomaniac on this earth! You didn't want to be bothered with anything—*anything*—that was going to get in the way of your precious acting——'

'Tell me once—just once—when you really tried and I didn't listen!'

'I'll tell you when I gave up,' she said with icy intensity. This was hurting more than she could have believed. 'It was the last time I saw you! I'd cried half the night before, in that horrible cold little bathroom in the lodgings we were in—and you never even noticed. And that was after I'd spent nearly three weeks trying to get one simple message through to you.'

If I'd had even half the attention you're giving me now, she thought bitterly, things might have been very different. His dark eyes were unreadable, but he never took them from her face. She forced herself to go on.

'We were in a cheap coffee bar, having lunch. I looked at you. I thought, "If he doesn't listen to me this time I don't know what I'm going to do." I had no friends there, and no one I could tell. I didn't know what your reaction was going to be—except that it couldn't be good.'

He said nothing. There was no way he could deny it, and he knew it. The Hal of five years ago had been everything she said. After his initial reaction, of course, things might have been different, but then she would have been responsible for ruining his prospects, and underneath he would have resented it. But she didn't want to talk about that now.

It was as though every detail of that last meeting had been etched on her memory with acid—even to the pattern of grain in the wooden table top they had sat at.

'I wanted to buy a train ticket home to see my parents,' she continued, her voice devoid of emotion. Now that she had actually got to the revelation she had feared, it was as though she was living in some dream—it didn't seem real at all. 'I didn't mean them to know about the baby, but I wanted money and a break—time in which to think. You were angry—when I tried to tell you about the baby, you got annoyed by. . .by something in the café.' She couldn't bring herself to remind him of his unintentionally cruel words now. He had never really meant them; it was one of those awful ironies of life that they had had such far-reaching consequences. 'You didn't understand why I needed to see my parents, and you were cross about the train ticket. You said we had no money. Then you talked about your audition that was coming up in Bristol in a couple of days, and how vital it was to you. You wanted to discuss your audition pieces with me, but you never even noticed when I wasn't listening.

'That afternoon I took a train to London, and another home to Sussex. All the way there I kept thinking how scared I was. We hadn't any money, we weren't married, and the last thing you wanted was a child. I thought that if my parents would only lend me some money, it might solve some of the problems. Eventually, I told my mother about the baby, instead of you.'

He seemed to have forgotten he still had hold of her wrist, and his grasp hadn't relaxed. She stared down now at his encircling fingers, and slowly he released her and withdrew his hand. The white marks turned to angry red on her skin.

'Was that when your parents wouldn't let me see you?'

'Yes. Possibly. I'd told you where I was going, but I never knew you had tried to see me, or even written, until you told me last summer.'

'So you thought——'

'What does it matter now what I thought?' she interrupted wearily. 'I don't suppose it could have changed anything. My parents were furious with you, and with me. They thought that by becoming involved with you in the first place I'd messed up my life. Then they weren't sure what to do for the best. After a while, they decided it would be a good idea if I went away. I went to stay with a cousin of my mother's near the Welsh Borders. . .about as obscure as you could get,' she added bitterly.

Emma had been elderly, and a kind enough woman in her way, but she hadn't been able to hide her disapproval of Nina's unmarried state. And then there had been her parents' all too visible struggle between concern for their daughter, and fear of scandal. Her mother had visited her several times, but the memory of those visits was still too painful to explore.

'What. . .happened to the child?' For the first time he sounded unsure of himself, as though he didn't quite know how to cope with what she was telling him.

'My mother at first suggested terminating the pregnancy. She thought it would be best for everyone in the long run. I refused.' She was deliberately leaving out bits of the story, remembering long hours of bitter discussion and argument, and her mother crying. And how she had cried and fought to keep the child who seemed by then the only link she had left with Hal. But she wasn't going to tell him that now; it had long been too late for his sympathy

Her mother had refused to let her have any money, believing, correctly, that she would have gone back to Hal if she could—until, of course, she had believed he had made no effort to contact her. Her parents would support her, but only if she did as they wished.

'Nina——!' He sounded agonised.

'You've asked me, so I'm going to tell you,' she interrupted coldly. 'I don't want to hear now what you think, or what I should have done! It's easy to be wise after the event. I did what seemed the only possible thing in the circumstances.'

Now that, at last, she had come to the moment to admit that burden of guilt she had carried about with her for so long, she found that it was not so difficult a thing to say. She no longer wanted to hurt Hal, only to get it over with; to put between them that final barrier—something he would never be able to bring himself to forgive her for.

'Before he was born, I agreed to hand him over for

adoption.' She paused. Hal said nothing. But it was worse than she'd thought, now she'd said it. She took a deep breath to stop her voice from betraying what was inside her. 'When you have no money, and no job, and none of your friends is in a position to help you, you have no power against parents like mine. . .but to be fair to them,' she continued with an effort, 'they did what they genuinely believed would be best for me. I knew that even then.'

'And the child?' Hal's voice was very low, and he never took his eyes off her.

'I. . .was ill. The baby was born six weeks early. He was very weak—he couldn't have lived. The doctors said it was respiratory failure. I never went back home again after that—I think my mother died believing I hated her. I still see my father. Possibly he wonders sometimes if what he did was right. But you can't go back—over anything.'

When Hal finally spoke, his voice was quiet but it gave nothing away about his real feelings. 'I'm sorry about your mother—and I know the way your parents felt about me, but did it never occur to you once after you'd gone that I might try to contact you?'

'I thought we'd discussed all that last summer.'

'OK—so your mother wouldn't let you receive my calls or my letters—but *you* could have rung, or written! Didn't you think I might have some sort of interest in a child that was mine? Doesn't a father have any rights?'

She was hurting so much that all her pain and bitterness came out in an overwhelming desire to wound. '*You* had rights, Hal? *You*? You sacrificed any rights you ever had to your ambition!' She thought he might strike her then, the look on his face was so terrible.

She could have told the story very differently—trying to win his sympathy and understanding, instead of alienating him. But the hard fact of the matter was that she had been prepared to give away his child without letting him have a chance to fight for it, and he would surely resent that underneath, even if he thought he could forgive her.

Her original motives had been basically unselfish: he would have had to make a choice between her and his career, and if he had chosen her, she would have made his future impossible. But he had had the right to make the choice, and she had denied him that right. And her only reason for telling him now was to drive him away, for good. It had been no more than a delusion, imagining that they both might have changed enough to have some sort of future together. They hadn't. They could still tear each other apart, just as they had been doing for the last hour.

'You've had what you came for, Hal. Now please leave.' Her voice, completely under control now, was expressionless, and she tried to keep her face blank. 'There is no future for us. There never can be. We finished five years ago.'

'And what if I don't agree?'

'You have no choice.' Again she was taking the decision out of his hands; this time there could be no question that she was right. 'I don't want you here now, or ever again. I want the peace and quiet that I had until you came back into my life last July. We'll destroy each other as lovers, and because we've been lovers we can't be friends.' It was then that the doorbell rang.

He looked instantly at his watch. 'Hell—that can't be.'

Nina got up and went to the door. She recognised

Nick on the doorstep. 'Hal and I are going up to Manchester together——' he began, and then faltered, looking at her cold, expressionless face. 'I—I haven't called at an inconvenient moment, have I? There was a phone call an hour ago, and we'll have to get a move on if we're going to get up there in time for the rehearsal.'

She let the implications of the word 'rehearsal' go. 'No,' she said, 'it's quite all right. We'd just finished.'

Hal had got up and followed her through from the kitchen. 'Just give us another five minutes, Nick——'

'I don't think we need them, do you?' she asked tonelessly. 'We've said about everything there is to say. Goodbye, Hal. Goodbye, Nick—it was nice to meet you while you were here. I hope you get to Manchester in time for your rehearsal.'

Nick, judging by his embarrassment, must have been briefed in advance by Hal. He looked as though he didn't quite know what to say or do, and was aware that he had interrupted some sort of row.

Hal was looking at her. She couldn't read the expression on his face, or the look in those dark eyes, but she sensed his anger. But it didn't matter now. Nothing mattered.

Then he said, 'Come on, Nick.'

She was aware that Nick had said some sort of a polite farewell, but her eyes were on the tall, bearded figure as he climbed into the passenger seat of the powerful Porsche, and then his companion started the engine.

She closed the door and went into the kitchen. It was windy and cold outside. There were dead leaves on the small lawn again. She'd have to rake them up or they'd spoil the grass. It was a pity chrysanthemums looked so ragged once the rain had got them. Her mind, completely detached, was working on irrelevant details. Inside she felt as though something had just crushed her, so that there was now nothing left of her real self at all.

She did the washing-up.

Later that afternoon there was a ring at the door. She had been looking through the accounts, concentrating determinedly on figures which meant little to her. Accounts were the best distraction she knew from any of those things that had happened only a few hours ago, and which she never wanted to think of again.

She got up. It was Jenny.

'Thank goodness you've answered the door,' she said. 'I've just had a very weird phone call and I'm here obeying instructions.' She looked worried.

'Oh?'

'Hal rang from a motorway café somewhere. He seemed in a hurry but he said that I was to get round here straight away, and that you needed company.'

Hal!—she thought she must have succeeded in making him hate her. Now what was he trying to prove? 'I'm perfectly all right,' Nina replied as coolly as she could manage. 'I can't imagine why he should think that.'

Jenny eyed her carefully. 'You don't look perfectly all right to me.'

'Hal and I had a row, that's all. And I deliberately tried to make him hate me. This is probably his idea of revenge—making you worried so that I feel guilty.'

Jenny brushed past her into the hall. 'Don't be ridiculous, Nina! Hal's one of the nicest men I've ever met—and he's absolutely crazy about you. You've only got to walk into the same room and he can't take his eyes off you.' Jenny's own hazel eyes were now full of concern. 'I don't know what sort of end-of-the-world row you two think you've had, but he was in quite a state—he thought you'd be into whisky and Mogadon cocktails in a big way. Get your coat—you're coming home with me. You don't look as though you ought to be left alone.'

Nina began to protest. 'I'm all right, Jenny, really——'

Her friend gave a half-smile. 'OK, then look at it this way—you're doing me a favour. Ed doesn't like me wasting food, and I've over-catered.'

Nina didn't know whether to smile or cry. It was typical of Jenny to think of some way of asking her that would suggest it was she who was doing them the favour.

'I'm not taking no for an answer,' Jenny said decisively. 'I'll give you five minutes to get ready. The car's outside.'

Later they peeled potatoes together in Jenny's kitchen, while Ed and Timmy watched television in the sitting-room. They'd been pretending to talk about recipes, when Jenny suddenly said, 'So you've had a row with Hal—want to talk about it?'

Nina looked at her. It wasn't fair to burden Jenny with that kind of confidence, but something prompted her to say, with no attempt at an introduction, 'I had Hal's child. And it died—and I never told him until this morning. Now we've got nothing more to say to each other.'

And, just then, even her friend's expression of shocked sympathy didn't disturb her—she felt strangely calm, detached. There, in Jenny's untidy kitchen, she decided that she would never feel anything again. She had no words and no tears.

It was finally finished.

CHAPTER NINE

'KNOW what I think?' Ed said conversationally. 'I think you ought to take a day off. Cambridge's most dynamic tutorial agency is hardly going to fall apart if you spend a few hours enjoying yourself.'

Nina looked up from the word processor. 'Are you talking about celebrating your pulling off that French deal?' she asked. She knew he wasn't, but she wanted to side-track him.

'That's not a bad idea, either.' He looked at her shrewdly. 'But it wasn't what I had in mind. We could of course take a couple of hours to have an illicit lunch in some local hostelry, but we'd spend the time talking business. No—I meant you need a break. Jenny says you're looking ill.' He examined her critically. 'Can't say I see it myself. I thought you were never looking better. She said that's what she meant. Typical woman's logic.'

For the past couple of weeks, she had taken unusual trouble with her appearance—she had certainly never worn so much make-up. Just because she worked at home, she told herself, that was no excuse to get sloppy. But underneath that superficial reasoning she had to admit that it was more and more of a mask for that terrible emptiness she had had inside since Hal had gone out of her life.

'Why not go down to London?' Ed suggested. 'Not many shopping days left till Christmas. Buy now or the shops'll be empty. . . I must be cracking under the strain myself, talking like a "Clichés for Foreigners" exercise.'

Ed was in a good mood these days. The results of his negotiations with the French language school were better than either of them could have hoped. It meant a lot more preliminary work arranging accommodation for the students at Easter, and Nina had found herself becoming a full-time secretary, while Ed had handled the day-to-day running of the agency.

She thought about his suggestion. She had got a lot of shopping to do. She was spending Christmas with him and Jenny, and was looking forward to hunting for interesting and amusing presents; she was always generous in her gifts, and loved thinking up surprises.

Up to now she had been glad of all the extra paperwork—it had stopped her brooding. But its effectiveness as a distraction was beginning to wear off. Also, the shock of her last encounters with Hal had had an anaesthetising effect on her feelings, and now that was wearing off too. Every day the dull ache of emptiness increased just a little more. It was becoming harder and harder to persuade herself that what she was doing had meaning at all. At the back of everything was the image of Hal as she had last seen him—hurt and angry, on the other side of the barrier she had done her best to put forever between them.

She hadn't expected to hear from him. She hadn't wanted it. He would have been a week in Manchester, rehearsing during the day, performing at night. Nick's reference to the rehearsal hadn't been lost on her—it could mean only one thing: Hal had made his decision and wasn't going to give up acting. But she couldn't believe that he hadn't cast aside his other ambitions: he had been planning to turn her into that home-maker and faithful wife he so wanted, until she had effectively destroyed any such ideas about herself forever.

He had been going with the company straight on to Birmingham, and finally to London for the end of the run. He must be in London this week, she thought. Well, that needn't make any difference to her. There were seven million people in London. The chances of her bumping into him among the Christmas shoppers were virtually non-existent.

She worked hard through Wednesday and Thursday to clear most of the letters. She often got up during the nights now, and came down to the office. It was a way of getting through the long, sleepless hours. She didn't know which was worse—lying there endlessly trying not to think, or falling into exhausted sleep just before dawn, only to dream in a series of violent, disjointed images that left her feeling tired and ill.

Increasingly, the sense of loss grew upon her. She couldn't escape the idea that somehow she might have been given a second chance. Perhaps, instead of the inevitable break between them and renewed pain that she had foreseen, there might have been the possibility of bridging that gap in both their lives and healing the wounds that they had inflicted on each other, as Hal himself had wanted.

Too often he was in her mind. She didn't think of their last agonising meeting, but of the times they had enjoyed together, even recently, and the trivial, undramatic aspects of their lives. Hal at the tutors' party, chatting easily with everyone he met, smiling over the heads of the guests once or twice, directly at her. The way he got on so well with her closest friends, fitting into the pattern as though he had always been part of it. She thought of him story-telling at Tim's school, walking with her pushing her bike that night after supper with Ed and Jenny, and kissing her under the lamp-post. She tried not to dwell on what she had felt in his arms the night he had made love to her. She had been a fool to condemn life with him as one perpetual drama: those moments had been the gentle hills and valleys of the ordinary, peaceful existence she longed for—and she had deliberately sent him away.

Yes, they had the power to destroy each other still. He could still hurt her more than she had ever thought possible, and she could hurt him, as she had done deliberately that last awful morning. She had tried to make him hate her—perhaps she had succeeded—but surely nothing could be more destructive to both of them than this terrible emptiness, this life with no real future.

What she was living now was only half an existence, and without Hal it would never be more than that. . . By the time she got on the train for London on Friday morning, she had made up her mind.

Sheer cowardice prevented her from ringing the theatre. Hal might be in a rehearsal, and she could have arranged to see him afterwards. If he wasn't, at least the theatre would have known where to contact him. He'd never told her the address of his flat in London—but, in any case, she lacked the courage to contact him at home. She was far too unsure of her reception.

She dithered round the West End in the vicinity of the theatre for hours, but never once did she see a man even remotely resembling the tall, bearded Elizabethan pirate he always looked to her.

She had a cup of tea in a snack bar, and ate a biscuit half-heartedly. She hadn't eaten all day, but she felt slightly sick. As it grew later, she wondered what to do. She could catch a train home, and maybe try to ring him tomorrow. . .but it would be commuter rush-hour soon. The Cambridge trains would be packed.

She could wait around until his performance finished, and then try to see him, but that would mean she still had hours to kill. . . . She could at least go along to the theatre and find out when the play ended.

It was *Hamlet*. There were pictures of Hal all over the front of the theatre. She bought a ticket, still unsure whether she would use it; but at least it gave her the option of how to spend the evening—if she had the courage. She was longing to see him, and frightened of the consequences. But this time he need never know she had been there, and if she walked out and went home there was no danger of him following her.

Once again, it was a deeply moving experience, but so different from that other time. She didn't make the mistake now of confusing the man with the stage role he played, and she was unexpectedly impressed by the maturity of his talent, and the depth of his understanding and sensitivity. The words he spoke were another man's, but the intelligence and controlled emotion that gave them meaning were Hal's. He might be playing a part, but, with every word, every action, he was revealing something of himself.

The audience, too, was completely held by him, and the performance ended in a stunned silence, delaying the storm of applause which followed. The death of Hamlet in the play had brought with it a profound sense of loss, but for her that sensation was mingled with a very real personal fear that had nothing to do with a character on the stage.

She watched Hal taking curtain calls with the rest of the cast. They looked tired and pleased. Hal smiled, but his expression was distant. It was as though his body only was present, acknowledging the acclaim. Hal himself was really somewhere else.

She had discovered the stage door during her earlier indecisive wanderings. Now, trying to suppress a feeling of panic, she found her way out of the theatre and round by a side-street to the back. There were groups of theatre-goers even here, making their way to taxis and tube stations, and some to restaurants. It was cold and late, but there was still a sense of liveliness and bustle.

She watched half a dozen schoolgirls chattering excitedly at the stage door. They were waiting for 'Hamlet' to come out. They *had* to get his autograph, and those of a couple of other young men in the cast.

Nina withdrew to the opposite pavement. She would go home—the whole thing was far too public. She should have rung Hal earlier. If she waited much longer she'd miss her train. But she just wanted one glimpse of him.

At last, some of the cast filtered through; some, grinning, signed programmes, while others slipped away unobtrusively. Hal came out with one of the actresses, and was immediately mobbed. He was dressed casually, as though he had been at a rehearsal, with a dark, heavy jacket and jeans. He smiled, and signed everything that was put in front of him, and joked with one or two of the stage-struck worshippers, but he looked tired.

He said something to the woman with him, and she nodded and moved away. Nina recognised Don just behind them. Perhaps they were going off to eat somewhere. She would have to go. She turned to take the shortest way back along the street to the tube station. Then she thought she heard him call her name.

She glanced back to see him scattering the schoolgirls to right and left, and quickly checking for traffic before he darted across the road to seize her by her elbow.

'Nina! Stop! What the hell are you doing here?' His eyes looked very bright in the street light, and he seemed so tall and unexpectedly real that he took her breath away. He was breathing quickly, and caught her upper arms to pull her against him as they were jostled by a passing group.

'I came to see the play,' she said, when she at last found her voice.

'I was thinking of you.' That wonderful voice was already sending shivers up her spine and his eyes held hers. 'But I never dreamed you'd actually be here!' He stopped, as though unsure of how to go on. 'What. . .why did——?' His fingers gripped her arms. Then he grinned, and the old teasing note came back into his voice. 'You came to see Don Garrod—I told you he had the best reviews of any of us!' But she knew he understood exactly why she was there.

Then he was looking down at her, as though unable to believe the evidence of his eyes and hands—as though he hardly knew what to say to her. . .

'I came for *you*,' she admitted, smiling. 'You were wonderful Hal! I'm so glad you didn't decide to give up the stage. . .' Then she paused, uncertain how to go on.

'I've had a long, long wait for this,' he said, unevenly, and pulled her into his arms.

Don, catching sight of Hal suddenly wrapping himself round the striking-looking silver-haired wraith on the opposite pavement, called out, 'Looks as though he's lost interest in supper!'

Nina felt Hal's laughter against her. Her face was

buried in his coat, and she could hardly breathe. She felt as though she was going to float away from sheer happiness. He was kissing her hair, and trying to kiss her ear, and he was still laughing.

She was vaguely aware of more good-natured remarks aimed in their general direction, and someone saying, 'Come on, for heaven's sake, before we starve!' There was some excited commentary from the groups of schoolgirls, and then Don's voice called out, 'Top of St Martin's Lane, Hal!'

He didn't reply, pulling her with him into the shadow of a dark doorway. Then his voice was rough as he spoke in her ear. 'Don't say *anything*. I don't want any "if"s or "but"s or explanations—I just want *now*. Five and a half years is a lifetime.'

One hand tangled in her hair, as he forced her to back up against the side of the doorway, his legs either side of hers. He pulled her head back, but she gave her lips to him willingly, her heart singing, feeling him press his body hard against hers, and anchor himself against her with one arm drawn tightly round her waist. His tongue probed her mouth, and she felt the movement of those slim, powerful hips against hers almost as though he couldn't help himself.

She was melting against him, into him, and the demand of his mouth on hers stung with a fierce, sweet fire. Love, in the guise of intense desire, washed through her. Involuntarily she arched more closely against him, while his mouth on hers deepened the kiss, its demand increasingly explicit. She wanted him more urgently with every second that passed.

Then she remembered where they were. She pushed at him feebly, gasping for breath, and feeling his breathing hard and uneven against her. 'Hal—stop it! Not here. . .We can't!' Somewhere in what was left of her mind, she was aware that famous actors didn't conduct their affairs in doorways, unless they wanted to make the very worst sort of headlines.

'Where, then?' His mouth was on her throat and his teeth grazed her skin. 'I'm not letting you go.'

She tried to ease some of the tension. 'Just as well,' she said breathlessly. 'I'd fall over.'

He drew a deep, shuddering breath, trying to still the raging pulses of his body. Then he buried his face in her hair and forced himself to hold her gently.

The feel of his arms, his hands, his strength was heaven. Half laughing, she put her lips to his ear. 'I know now exactly why couples make love in dark alleys!' she whispered. 'Do you think I ought to be thoroughly ashamed of myself?'

His arms tightened round her again, and he looked down at her. 'Don't you dare be ashamed of anything—*anything*! Do you understand what I'm telling you?'

She did. He was telling her that he didn't want her apologies for what had happened in Cambridge, or for anything that had happened between them before that. Just the fact of her being there like that had told him all he wanted to know, and, as far as he was concerned, everything that mattered had at last come miraculously right between them.

She slipped her hands into that wonderful strong, silky hair, to draw him down to her. 'I love you,' she said, and kissed him with all the love her secret heart had held for over five long years.

After a while, he raised his head to look down at her again. Much later, when she thought about what followed, she was almost amused that the most intimate and intensely romantic moment of her life had passed in a London back-street, in that dark doorway where there was litter under their feet.

'This is forever, isn't it?' Hal asked softly, and she nodded, unable to speak.

She didn't know how long they stood there, until at last a grin crept across Hal's handsome pirate face, and she saw the glitter of his eyes in the shadowed darkness of the doorway.

'Just tell me,' he said, 'have we got another audience?' She peered cautiously round his shoulder. People were still passing but the group of avid teenage onlookers had vanished. They were now only another couple in a doorway. Just as well, she thought with a wry grin: they had been close to writing an entire new act to *Hamlet*.

'Are you going to tell me what that last little smile was for?'

She withdrew her hands from under his jacket, and then caught sight of a dark stain on his shirt. Her hand was smeared with it. 'You've got blood on you!' she exclaimed, horrified.

He grinned at her. 'I know—it's from that sword-fight at the end of the play. Are you going to come home and minister to my collection of wounds for me?—most of them, I might add, inflicted by you at various stages of our acquaintance.'

She knew that he was teasing, but she also knew very well what sort of wounds he was referring to. She looked up at him, everything she felt clearly legible in her face, and, despite what he had said about apologies, she couldn't stop herself. 'Oh my darling, I'm so sorry. . .for everything. For leaving you the way I did—and for trying to hurt you the way I did.'

'Sweetheart, don't let's do this to each other—you've got just as much, if not more, to forgive me for.' Then that long, mobile mouth quirked into another smile. 'Would you rather we just called it quits and said goodbye here and now?'

For one second she stared at him in utter bewilderment, and then her expression changed. 'Hal Crayle, if you think I've come all the way here from Cambridge——!'

He was chuckling at her expression of mock outrage. 'I don't,' he said. 'I think you've come all the way here from Cambridge to go to bed with me. Haven't you?'

She couldn't remember the last time she'd blushed. He could probably see it even in the street lighting. He slung an arm round her shoulder, catching up her hand to interlink her fingers with his. They walked slowly, leaning slightly against each other, down towards the Strand. He matched his stride to hers. He'd parked his car in one of the back-streets towards the river.

'I've been praying for this every day for nearly three weeks—which includes two very black Sundays,' he said. I couldn't have got to see you even if I'd tried while we were on tour. I wanted to ring you, but what we had to say couldn't be talked about over the phone. I was hoping that you might come to your senses a bit earlier and decide that you couldn't live without me while I was in Manchester. . .'

'You arrogant——!'

His interruption was totally disarming. 'Ah, but Manchester would never have been the same again—Manchester, next best place to heaven on earth! Then, when you weren't there, I thought it'd have to be Birmingham that'd be suddenly transformed. And if it hadn't been London this week, I'd have made it Cambridge next—I couldn't wait any longer!'

She laughed. She couldn't have believed she could

feel so happy—but it was no dream this time. Everything was an intense reality.

Hal was still teasing. 'Haven't you noticed how London's totally different? There are even stars in the street.'

'Only if you're looking at the Christmas decorations!'

He stopped walking and turned her to face him, looking down into her eyes. 'No, I'm looking at them right now. . .'

'There was a time when I'd have thought you were being very insincere and theatrical if you'd said something like that!' she accused. 'And can this be the man who told me last summer that he was depressed because none of the words he said seemed to be his own?'

'Ah!' He gave a dramatic sigh. 'But I've discovered a secret—the words don't matter. It's the feelings behind them that make them real, and since I met you again I've had plenty of those—though I could have done without some of them! I tried every way I could think of to get through to you, and every time I thought I'd made it there was another blank wall. I knew you were hiding something, but I had no idea about the baby. . .' The teasing note in his voice had gone.

She put up her hand to his face, her fingers exploring the crisp, clear-cut lines of his beard. 'I didn't want to get involved because I couldn't risk losing you again,' she said quietly. 'It wasn't until I met you last summer that I realised just how much of my life had been missing up to then, and I didn't want to admit it.'

'And I thought you must hate me after that last row we had in Cambridge. It hurt at first to find out just how much you'd kept hidden from me—how little you'd trusted me——'

'But I didn't *want* to hurt you!' she broke in. 'That was why I wouldn't tell you until you didn't leave me any choice!'

'Hush,' he said. 'It was my own fault. I understand now, and I don't blame you. And I realised after I left you that morning that you were only telling part of the story. You'd chosen the words deliberately to make me angry, and left out everything that. . .' The deep, golden voice had roughened suddenly. 'You must have gone through hell before you left me five years ago. . .and after.'

'Hal——' she said quickly. 'The baby—can you really forgive me for not giving you the chance to decide his future?' Even now it cost something to ask the question, when she had dreaded for so long what the answer must be.

His arms tightened round her reassuringly. 'You were right—everything you said to me in Cambridge was true. I didn't deserve someone like you, Nina, and I don't blame your parents for what they did. I was utterly obsessed with my career and I did sacrifice everything—including you, although I couldn't see it at the time—to what I wanted. You've got nothing to be forgiven for, my love. You took the only way that was open to you. . .'

She slipped her arms round his neck, pulling him closer. 'I would have kept him, Hal—I wouldn't have given him up for anyone if. . .' But she couldn't go on.

He didn't say anything for a few moments, but she knew from the way he was holding her that he understood everything that she couldn't put into words just then.

'We'll have lots of babies,' he said softly, 'if that's what you want—enough to start a whole theatrical company!'

She had to smile. 'You were never one for modest aims in life, were you, Hal Crayle?'

His reply sounded suspiciously meek. 'I was a selfish, pig-headed, ambitious brute,' he said, 'but I did love you.'

'What do you mean, *did*?' she demanded.

'Do.' He put his arms round her briefly, and groaned. 'Come on. Let's go home before I have to make love to you on the pavement and we're found by a policeman.'

The car was in the next street. She looked down at the long, low power-machine that said 'HAL 1' on it—uncompromisingly self-advertising.

'I wonder,' she remarked, patently unimpressed, 'if this is the reward for being a selfish, pig-headed, ambitious brute in your youth? Because, if you fancy collecting any more success symbols, I'd appreciate it if you'd reconsider your manner of acquiring them.' They smiled at each other across HAL 1.

'After that pompous speech, I'll buy a bicycle!' he promised, and then held out a bunch of keys. 'Here—you drive. I'm getting distracted by my wound.'

Instantly she was horrified by her own thoughtlessness. 'Darling, I'm so sorry—how bad is it? Do you want a doctor to look at it?'

He climbed into the car, and all but lay in the passenger seat. 'I'll survive,' he said weakly. 'But if anybody's going to make any love tonight, you're going to have to be the active one.'

Confused visions of gaping wounds and doctors with yards of bandage distracted her. 'But Hal——' she started to protest. He was looking up at her from under those long, dark eyelashes as she hesitated with the keys, wondering if she should drive to the nearest hospital despite what he'd said.

'I seem to remember you were rather good at it.'

'Good at what?'

'Making love. That's the ignition.'

The glimmer of a suspicion crossed her mind even then, as she looked at him lying back in the seat, eyes closed, one arm tenderly laid across his ribs. But it wasn't until she got him back to the flat and virtually into bed that she discovered that it was stage blood.

So much, she reflected—with what was left of coherent thought once he had set out to prove that he was anything but a passive invalid—for her new-found theories on the sincerity of actors!

Only one small lamp glowed in the far corner of the big sitting-room, which was warm and shadowy in the flickering light of the fire. It was a beautiful room, skilfully combining comfort and a certain old-fashioned elegance. Nina had fallen in love not just with the room but with the whole house the instant she had seen it.

'If only you had brought me to St Albans instead of chasing me all over Cambridge!' she'd teased Hal when she'd first seen it. 'I'd have married you straight away!'

Jenny yawned, and wound up the knitting on her lap into a neat package. 'What time did you say Hal would be back?'

'After twelve—he never manages to get away from London as soon as he thinks. It's a pity Ed wasn't going to have time to see him there after his meeting with that French chap—and we haven't managed a weekend all together since before Juliet was born.'

'True——' Jenny agreed, 'but if people have to go off making films in places like New Zealand, and just at Christmastime too, what can you expect?'

Nina switched back to their first topic. 'At least the

agency's doing about as much business as it can handle now, even taking into account recent expansion. I'm so glad Ed's made such a spectacular success of it.'

'A lot of it is thanks to you, you know,' Jenny replied warmly. 'If you hadn't been so generous about keeping the house on and paying the running costs all the time you were in the States with Hal, Ed wouldn't have been able to take on any extra help.'

'Jen, you know you and Ed have been like family to me—and if it weren't for your support all that time when I'd met Hal again, Ed would have been stuck indefinitely with a very half-hearted business partner. It was the least I could do—and we are still partners in a way, so it's in my interests when he's making money!'

'Well, it's nice to see that you agreed in the end with my character assessment of Hal!' Jenny teased. 'Who'd have thought that in little over a year you'd be living such a glamorous lifestyle, with a famous husband—and a six-month-old baby? And there was Ed thinking that you'd only gone up to London for a few hours of Christmas shopping! He really is the original obtuse male!'

Then Nina laughed, remembering the look on Ed's face when one morning, well over a year ago now, and several days after she had set off on the so-called 'shopping expedition', she had walked into the office with Hal.

'My God!' Ed had exclaimed in mock outrage. 'That took you long enough! What on earth were you doing—buying up half of Regent Street? Hello, Hal—nice to see you. Brought the delinquent back, have you? Everything's been in chaos since she skived off—never been so busy.'

Nina, still somewhere on cloud nine, had slipped her arms round her husband of two days, and had smiled, leaning against him. 'Good try, Ed, but I happen to have been in touch with Jenny every day, and she assured me that I could have a couple of weeks off if I felt like it because you've never been so idle!'

'Well, maybe I haven't,' Ed had agreed with a rueful grin. 'But that's no excuse for you! What have you been up to?'

She had found her attempt at a reply cut off by Hal's hand unexpectedly clamped over her mouth.

'She got picked up in the street by a very doubtful man who is known to specialise in false identities, tricked into getting into his fast car, taken to his flat under false pretences, and then seduced. And that was only the beginning.' Hal had been holding her against him, mock gangster-style. 'Is she blushing yet? I can't see from this angle.'

Ed had been grinning from ear to ear. 'Only faintly pinkish!'

'Brazen hussy, isn't she? And I can't say she put up much of a fight. . .'

Nina had considered how the hand that was clamped across her mouth was soon—once she had given up her part in the agency—to be the hand that fed her. She had considered it. And then she had bitten it.

Now, as she smiled across at Jenny, remembering, she knew that never in her life had she been so happy. Just over a year ago she had wondered if there was anything worth living for, and now it was as though she had been given everything—gift-wrapped like all those presents she had finally got round to buying the day before she and Hal had left London.

Once Jenny had gone to bed, with apologies to the still absent Hal, Nina went upstairs to minister to a wailing Juliet and ended up bringing her down to the sitting-room in an attempt to pacify her. Then she sat for a long time by the fire with the baby in her arms. She liked waiting up for Hal, and, anyway, she couldn't sleep until she knew he was safely home. They had scarcely spent a night apart since their marriage.

She knew that they had both changed a great deal since those disastrous early days. She no longer felt insecure, or unsure of the nature of her relationship with him. She knew now that there was so much more between them than the physical passion which had carried her away at first, and caused her to be so wary later of renewing their relationship. And she had no sense now of being taken for granted while he got on with his more immediate concerns. She and Juliet were the centre of his life, just as he was hers.

Without each other, they had only been living half-lives, but he had been willing to acknowledge it far sooner than she. Now they had found a peace and security in each other—something they both craved—that were unaffected by the constantly changing external pattern of their lives. Marriage, and the birth of their daughter, had effectively laid the ghosts that had haunted her for too long.

It was after midnight when she heard Hal's key in the lock. Juliet, now tucked in between her and the back of the sofa on which she was lying stretched out with a book, was fast asleep.

She heard Hal pause in the hall, and then the sitting-room door was pushed open.

'You should have gone to bed,' he said softly. 'Keeping my daughter up till all hours.' He was still wearing his coat, and brought a breath of the cold March night in with him.

She smiled at him, inner happiness lighting up her eyes.

'Ed's had to stay in London, and Jenny says to

apologise for her lapse in manners but she just couldn't keep awake any longer. Did you and Don and Nick and whoever get to eat anything?' She kept her voice low, careful of waking Juliet.

He came to stand beside her, looking down at her, and traced the side of her face with one finger. 'You look beautiful lying there like that. . .' And then, 'So the Frog has got her own way again!'

'The Frog' was Hal's favourite nickname for his daughter. It might have been unflattering, but the tone of his voice did little to disguise the fact that he thought that the moon and stars revolved round her.

Nina, although she pretended to protest, did nothing to stop him as he took hold of the waistband of her jeans and pulled her up to stand beside him.

'I'm not tearing your clothes off you,' he said. He put his arms round her, pulling her close. 'And if I've done any damage to your jeans you can have another pair—as many pairs as you want.'

She was reminded, fleetingly, of the rows they had had, years ago—in another world it seemed—about money. And how it had been the lack of money that had parted them for what had felt like a lifetime. Now he never stopped giving her things. She sometimes wondered if he wasn't trying to make up for those early days, when poverty and ambition had taken their toll, and both she and Hal in their different ways had had to pay a heavy price.

'Well?' she asked, looking up at him. 'You never answered my question. Are we going to raid the kitchen?'

He kissed the tip of her nose. 'You and your midnight feasts. . .'

Later, they sat opposite each other at the kitchen table. Their conversations, as was habitual between them now, were easy and relaxed, and punctuated by companionable silences.

'Take your hands off my food!' he complained, grinning, and whipping the plate out of her reach. 'You eat your own chicken sandwiches. I haven't had anything all day.'

'Neither have I. What I really feel like is cake. I wonder if we've got any left after Timmy had a go at it?' She got up to prowl round the cake tins.

'Why didn't you have anything to eat?' he demanded after a pause, mouth full of sandwich. 'I've told you before I don't like skinny wives.'

She didn't reply, but she knew that he was watching her. She kept her back turned, to hide the half-smile that would give away something that she knew he already suspected. 'Want some jam roll?'

'No, thanks—are you sure you want that *and* chocolate cake?' And then, 'Come and sit next to me. Whenever I see you on the opposite side of the kitchen table I'm reminded of that awful breakfast when we tried to tear each other to shreds and very nearly succeeded.'

She sat on his knee and put one arm round his neck. 'Maybe we had to have that one final row so that we would never need to have another.'

'Then stop picking the best bits out of my chicken sandwiches if you want to keep it that way.'

'I wonder why the significant moments of our lives always seem to take place at mealtimes?' she asked, trying to sound off-hand.

Hal, finishing the remains of a crust, raised an enquiring eyebrow. 'And what exactly is so significant about this particular moment? Could it be something to do with the fact that you've had half a chocolate cake, the remains of a jam roll, two biscuits and an apple—not to mention the insides of my sandwiches? Or could it be that you've got a guilty secret and you're wondering how to tell me?'

'There's nothing guilty about it!' she protested, and then laughed.

'Oh, yes, there is,' he said softly. 'The very fact that you've got a secret at all. We promised each other *no* secrets—remember?'

She turned in his lap so that she could look him in the eyes. 'It can't be a secret, for two reasons,' she said firmly. 'First, I'm not sure of it myself yet, and second. . .you know it already!' They had come a very long way from that cheap café where, years ago, she had tried to tell him that she was having his child.

'How *do* you know?' she demanded, half laughing as he began to kiss her ear.

'Because you've got the same look in your eyes as last time. And less romantically, because you were eating that cake as if there was no tomorrow.'

'You don't think it's a bit soon for us to have another baby? You are pleased, aren't you?' She knew he was, but she needed to hear him say it.

Hal sighed, and raised his eyes to heaven. 'My darling,' he explained with heavy patience, 'haven't we agreed that we're going to be a famous theatrical family?'

'You could do one-man shows.'

He gave her one of his most piratical grins. 'Where's your imagination, woman? I want full-scale Shakespeare! And with more male parts than female on offer, it's about time you evened up the numbers!'

'You count for at least six men already, Hal Crayle. You're a selfish, pig-headed. . .er, what was it?'

'Ambitious brute,' he supplied promptly. 'But——'

'You do love me?'

'Yes,' he said.

Zodiac Wordsearch
Competition

How would you like a years supply of Mills & Boon Romances ABSOLUTELY FREE?

Well, you can win them! All you have to do is complete the word puzzle below and send it into us by Dec 31st 1990. The first five correct entries picked out of the bag after this date will each win a years supply of Mills & Boon Romances (Six books every month - worth over £100!) What could be easier?

S	E	C	S	I	P	R	I	A	M	F
I	U	L	C	A	N	C	E	R	L	I
S	A	I	N	I	M	E	G	N	S	R
C	A	P	R	I	C	O	R	N	U	E
S	E	I	R	A	N	G	I	S	I	O
Z	O	D	W	A	T	E	R	B	R	I
O	G	A	H	M	A	T	O	O	A	P
D	R	R	T	O	U	N	I	R	U	R
I	I	B	R	O	R	O	M	G	Q	O
A	V	I	A	N	U	A	N	C	A	C
C	E	L	E	O	S	T	A	R	S	S

Pisces	Aries	Leo	Earth
Cancer	Gemini	Virgo	Star
Scorpio	Taurus	Fire	Sign
Aquarius	Libra	Water	Moon
Capricorn	Sagittarius	Zodiac	Air

Please turn over for entry details

How to enter

All the words listed overleaf, below the word puzzle, are hidden in the grid. You can can find them by reading the letters forwards, backwards, up and down, or diagonally. When you find a word, circle it, or put a line through it. After you have found all the words, the left-over letters will spell a secret message that you can read from left to right, from the top of the puzzle through to the bottom.

Don't forget to fill in your name and address in the space provided and pop this page in an envelope (you don't need a stamp) and post it today. Competition closes Dec 31st 1990.

Only one entry per household (more than one will render the entry invalid).

Mills & Boon Competition
Freepost
P.O. Box 236
Croydon
Surrey CR9 9EL

Hidden message ______________________________

____

Are you a Reader Service subscriber. **Yes** ❑ **No** ❑

Name ______________________________

Address ______________________________

____

____

______________________________ **Postcode** ______________________________

You may be mailed with other offers as a result of entering this competition.
If you would prefer not to be mailed please tick the box. No ❑

COMP9